JULIA DURANGO
TYLER TERRONES

An Imprint of HarperCollinsPublishers

HarperTeen is an imprint of HarperCollins Publishers.

Library of Congress Control Number: 2017934822
ISBN 978-0-06-231403-1

Typography by Torborg Davern
17 18 19 20 21 PC/LSCH 10 9 8 7 6 5 4 3 2 1

First Edition

In memory of our grandmothers:

Adele Pollard
Shirley Terrones
Mary Frances Greider
& Marion Mack Holloway

For raising the best people we know.

ONE

WE'VE ALL HAD THAT ONE DREAM.

No, not the one where your teeth crumble and fall out of your head, and you desperately try to catch the shards of bicuspids, incisors, and shattered molars in your hands, to no avail.

Not the one where you can fly or where you wake up right before you hit the ground. Those are kind of exciting.

And no, not *that* one either. My head isn't that far in the gutter.

I'm talking about the other one. The one where you're suddenly in school wearing nothing but your underwear. Where the hell are your pants? And why the hell is no one noticing?

That dream.

I've had it regularly since kindergarten, and it's never any fun. I don't even wear underwear in real life. I mean, I don't go *commando*—I wear boxer briefs, to be specific—but why am I always wearing the damn tightie-whities in that dream?

You know the only good part about that dream, though? It's the enormous relief you feel when you wake up and consciousness washes over you like a warm, soothing wave. Even as you stumble into your mundane, everyday life filled with alarm clocks, midterms, and your crazy family—and my family's crazier than most, believe me—at least you're wearing pants.

But pants or no pants, those dreams were nothing compared to how bad my real life had been going.

It had been exactly forty-seven days since Mom had uprooted me and my little brother, Grub, from our lifelong home in Chicago and transplanted us a hundred miles west to the small town of Buffalo Falls, aka Nowhere, Illinois.

Seriously, it's *small*. Like, one high school, two supermarkets, three burger joints, six churches, and eight bars small. Plus, one brand-spanking-new vegetarian café, owned and operated by none other than my mom, Coriander Gunderson. Free delivery all summer between eleven and two!

That's right, after being the new kids at school one month before summer break, my eight-year-old brother and I had been tasked with the "free delivery" part of my mom's new business venture. Mom insisted Grub needed "fresh air and new scenery" every day and would be a "good little helper." Apparently, she's a little hazy on child labor laws, workers' rights, and occupational safety hazards.

Which is how, the second week of June, I happened to be pedaling across town on her old Schwinn bike with Grub standing on the foot pegs behind me. No waking up from that nightmare.

As always, Grub wore a plastic green army helmet, a camouflage vest over his T-shirt and shorts, and a Nerf bazooka strapped to his back. His little claws dug into my shoulders as I pedaled through town, making salad deliveries.

As we crossed the bridge over the Stone River to the south side of Buffalo Falls, some guy must have noticed our thirst, because he graciously offered us a blue Slurpee out the window of his convertible Jeep Wrangler.

By offered, I mean he winged it at us.

It splattered to our left, spraying cold, sticky sugar water all over our legs. He may have yelled "Losers!" out the window too, but I couldn't hear him over the music playing through my earbuds.

"Fire in the hole!" yelled Grub, which I *did* hear since he was only two inches from my head.

My brother's real name is Manuel (pronounced man-WELL, not MAN-you-el), but I've called him Grub as long as I can remember. I don't know why. He's always looked like a little grub, I guess. A little Puerto Rican–Norwegian grub.

That's right, he's a Puertowegian.

Never heard of a Puertowegian? No surprise. That's probably because one hasn't ever existed in the history of, well, ever.

Except for my World War II–obsessed brother, Manuel Thor Gunderson.

If you think his name is bad, get a load of mine: Jesús Bjorn Gunderson (hey-ZOOS bee-YORN). I know what you're thinking. Another Puertowegian, right?

Wrong.

I have the honor to be Mexiwegian. I think that sounds better than Norwexican. Yep, I'm half Mexican, half Norwegian, like a lutefisk taco. Apparently my mom has a thing for Latin men. Unlike Grub, though, all of my mom's Norwegian features were downloaded into my DNA, so I look more Bjorn than Jesús.

But everyone calls me Zeus.

I'm pretty average looking, I guess. Brown hair, blue eyes, fair skin, 145 pounds. I'm trying to grow sideburns, but so far it looks more like someone glued random hair plugs to my face.

At the moment, though, I was bright red, trying to get the bike ride from hell over as quickly as possible. Grub and I recovered from the Slurpee grenade and made our way up the hill. The director of Hilltop Nursing Home had recently signed up for the 5-Day Deal. It was a coupon special my mom had come up with to attract business to her new shop, the World Peas Café. That day's deal? Make Quinoa, Not War.

I told you my mom was terrible with names.

For the past few weeks, I'd mainly been delivering to downtown business owners, "downtown" referring to the little collection of buildings surrounding a shady park. The nursing home would be our first venture across the bridge to the south side of town.

Following my phone's map app, we turned right at the next stoplight, then a left, then another right into a residential area. The tidy-looking homes on either side of the street provided a stark contrast to the ramshackle houses in our own neighborhood where we rented a ground-level apartment.

Hilltop Nursing Home finally appeared—you guessed it—at the top of the hill, and holy hell, it was huge. Buffalo Falls must have a surplus of old people. And the old-people business must be booming, because this place looked like Buckingham Palace. Not that I'd ever been there, but Jesus (JEE-zus).

A sea of lawn surrounded the castle-like structure.

"Drop-off point at nine o'clock!" Grub yelled in the best army voice an eight-year-old can muster.

You know how I mentioned Grub is obsessed with World War II? That's putting it mildly. Not only had he spent the last few years having Nerf gun fights with his friends in our old Chicago neighborhood, but he could give you a detailed breakdown of the Battle of the Bulge *and* Operation Overlord. By the time he was seven, he'd checked out every volume on World War II history the Chicago Public Library had to offer. He was too young to read them cover to cover, of course, but he loved studying the pictures and maps.

I know, I know, what mother would allow her little boy to

immerse himself in that kind of violence and bloodshed? That would be our peace-loving, antiwar mom, Coriander Gunderson, who also doesn't believe in "shielding her children from hard truths." As long as Grub and I were reading and not staring at a screen, she gave us free rein among the library shelves.

I chained the bike to a bench, and Grub and I headed to the arched entryway of Hilltop Nursing Home. I carried the cardboard salad container—100 percent recycled material, mind you—while Grub dove and tumbled behind me, avoiding imaginary machine gun fire and mortar explosions.

The glass doors opened automatically as we approached, and a wave of nursing-home odor smacked me right in the olfactory receptors.

Now—*disclaimer*—I have nothing against old people. In fact, I hope to be one someday. But we all know that nursing-home odor. It's like if you bottled up the smell of a hospital, added a splash of grade-school cafeteria, then threw in a little diarrhea, and tried to cover it up with Lysol.

Grub commando-crawled past me into the lobby. I heard someone playing the piano in the distance.

Grub ducked beneath a nearby reception desk, Nerf bazooka at the ready. "All clear, Sarge!" he shouted.

Do you know one good thing about nursing homes? Old people love little kids like they love their hard candies. That means it's nearly impossible to be embarrassed by your little brother "playing army," Grub's favorite game.

I approached the lady at the reception desk.

"Hi, are you here to visit someone?" she asked.

"No, actually I'm making a delivery to . . ." I checked the receipt again. "Missy Stouffer."

The woman glanced down at a day planner. "Ms. Stouffer is in a meeting right now, but if you'd like to have a seat in the common room, she'll be with you shortly." She pointed down the hall.

"Thanks," I said, then turned to Grub. "Let's move, Private."

"Sir, yes, sir!" he shouted, barrel-rolling past me to clear the path of enemies.

As we made our way, the piano music got louder and louder. What was that song? It had an old-time, dreamy feel to it. It reminded me of the Beatles for some reason, but I couldn't place it.

The hallway opened up into a large room, where a crowd of white-haired, wrinkly people sat in various armchairs and sofas around a black grand piano, nodding and tapping in time to the music.

As the final chords resonated through the room, the crowd burst into applause, and I glanced over at the piano player. I was expecting some old guy to be sitting there, but I couldn't have been more wrong.

Instead, it was the girl who changed everything.

TWO

EVER GET CAUGHT STARING AT SOMEONE? IT'S STRANGE HOW FROM across a room, forty feet away, you can tell when you've made direct eye contact. How big is the pupil in the human eye anyway, a few millimeters? Isn't it crazy that we can tell when someone else's millimeter-sized dot of blackness is directly lined up with our own? I don't know about you, but when this happens to me, I find the best approach is to suddenly jerk my vision a few degrees away, and act as if I've just seen the most interesting thing in the universe.

That's exactly what I did when the piano girl looked up at me. I don't know if it's because I was caught by surprise, or if I had a mild Lysol high, but I completely panicked. First of all, she was smoking hot, and I mean that with all due respect and admiration. Shiny black hair. Dark eyes. Coppery skin. Dimples. Yellow sundress. A thin silver chain around her neck that made me realize just how inviting a collarbone could be. Second of all, she looked to be my age. Third, and possibly most important, whatever that song was, she'd played it like a pro, without any music in front of her. The melody still lingered in my brain, taunting me with its familiarity.

I stood there frozen in the middle of the hallway, salad in one hand, receipt in the other, and stared at a spot on the wall like the world's lamest statue.

Thankfully, the moment was interrupted by the cackling of an old woman in the crowd. "Enough of this sappy shit, Cupcake! How 'bout some Tom Jones!"

I looked back over to Hot Piano Girl for a reaction and—get this—she smiled at me. My brain said, "Smile back," but my gut said, "Look back at that spot on the wall."

Hot Piano Girl then went into what must have been a song by Tom Jones, for Cackling Woman hopped up—pretty spryly, I might add—snapped her fingers over her head, and started singing: *"Well she's all you'd ever want, she's the kind I like to flaunt and take to dinner..."* Some of the neighboring residents sang along, while others slept through the performance. A man in the far corner rose from his wheelchair, put a hand over his heart, and in his best tenor started belting out, *"O say can you seeeeee..."*

I remained frozen in the hallway, in awe of the spectacle.

I dared to look back at Hot Piano Girl.

She smiled again.

I smiled back this time but screwed the whole thing up. Imagine school-photo day, when your smile doesn't reach your eyes. I immediately wished I had thought of something cooler to do. Hot Piano Girl motioned toward the crowd with her head and raised her eyebrows in amusement. I still had the cheesy smile on my face, but I couldn't take it off now, because she'd notice. So I continued smiling, and raised my eyebrows back at her, like a ventriloquist's dummy.

Suddenly, I snapped out of my hypnotic state, remembering I had an eight-year-old I was responsible for. I hadn't heard any battle cries since the Tom Jones song began, so I knew he must be hiding somewhere nearby.

"Grub?" I yelled.

Nothing.

"*Private* Grub, what's your twenty?" I called again.

"Behind the tree, sir," called his tiny voice from behind a potted plant.

"Copy that, carry on," I replied, relieved I hadn't lost him.

I looked back at Hot Piano Girl, who gave me the "d'awwww, that's adorable" face. I'm pretty sure my own face turned a dark shade of maroon, but for the first time all day, I began to feel glad I had my weird brother with me.

The moment was cut short when a nurse wheeled a big

skeleton of a man with a face like a bulldog around the corner. He looked like he was a hundred and fifty years old.

"Right behind you, soldier!" he shouted at Grub, whose plastic helmet peeked above the plant.

My brother paused for a moment, taking in the man's gray sweatshirt adorned with military patches and medals.

"Were you in the army?" Grub asked from behind the plant.

"Damn straight I was. Sergeant John Porter, Fifty-Ninth Artillery Regiment, G Battery. Fort Hughes, Philippines, World War II."

Grub's eyes widened—he'd never met anyone who'd actually fought in World War II before. Grub must have recognized the insignia of a superior officer, because he immediately hopped out from behind the plant and stood at attention. "Heavy action there, sir?"

Sergeant Porter snorted. "Got our asses handed to us in Corregidor. What's a little boy like you know about it?"

I took a step toward Grub at the man's harsh words, but the nurse behind him smiled at us reassuringly. She put a gentle hand on the man's shoulder. "Be nice, Blackjack. This little soldier's just curious."

The man eyeballed my brother for a moment and nodded. "At ease."

Grub's body relaxed. "I've read a lot of books, sir."

"Well, believe you me, I've got stories that's not in any books."

"Okay, Blackjack," the nurse said. "Time to say good-bye so we can listen to Rose."

"Rose who?" Blackjack asked, turning toward the nurse.

"My daughter, Rose. We listen to her play the piano every day after lunch."

"Right." The man lifted his chin and looked at Grub. "Keep an eye out, soldier. I'm goin' in."

"I got you covered," said Grub, repositioning himself behind the plant. He peeked out one last time. "Sir, would you tell me some of those stories sometime? The ones that aren't in any books?"

Blackjack grinned. "You bet."

I looked back to the girl named Rose playing piano, to find her watching me and laughing.

And wow, what a smile. I gave a stiff wave.

The place was really rocking now. A few of the female residents had coupled up to dance and were singing the repeating refrain: *"She's a lady . . . whoa, whoa, whoa, she's a lady!"*

Off in the corner, the national anthem met its climax as the tenor continued: *"And the rockets' red glare! The bombs bursting in air! Gave proof through the night, that our flag was still there."*

Then—and I couldn't make this up if I tried—the girl named Rose perfectly segued from Tom Jones to Francis Scott Key with a couple of chord changes.

The tenor took his cue: *"O say does that star-spangled banner yet waaaave . . . o'er the land of the freeee, and the home of the brave?"*

"To victory!" Blackjack shouted, raising a fist and grinning over his shoulder at the potted plant.

Grub raised a small fist in response.

The room broke into applause just as a woman in a black pantsuit rushed into the common room, typing away on her cell phone.

"Enemy, twelve o'clock!" shouted Blackjack. "Prepare to fire!"

The woman shot a quick glare at Blackjack's nurse.

Grub looked at Blackjack, then at me, as if he couldn't believe a grown-up was playing army with him.

I shrugged. Hell, I didn't know what was going on. My mind was still on the girl.

"Target locked," confirmed Grub, followed by *"BZSHOOO!"* which, I imagine, was the sound of the bazooka firing.

"Watch your crossfire!" yelled Blackjack.

"Target missed! I repeat, target missed!" shouted Grub.

"Retreat!" yelled Blackjack, his voice fading as the nurse quickly ushered him out of the room.

The woman in black marched straight toward me, never looking away from her phone. She was striking, in a sort of a sharp-businesswoman way, her hair pulled back into a tight bun. She held out cash between her first and second fingers without ever looking up.

"Missy Stouffer?" I asked.

"Ms. Stouffer, yes."

I checked the receipt. "Eight ninety-five."

She looked at me for the first time, over the top of her red-framed glasses. "And worth every penny, I'm sure."

"It's really good," I said. Truthfully, I'd never even tried it. But she didn't need to know that.

"I hope so," she replied, motioning with the cash for me to take it. She handed me two fives and told me to keep the change. I wanted to say, "Gee, thanks," but kept my mouth shut. Then Ms. Stouffer marched back from wherever she came.

As soon as she was gone, the room returned to life. Cackling Woman, clearly the pack leader, yelled, "More Tom Jones!" The girl named Rose went right into it, and several residents joined in for the chorus: *What's new, pussycat? Whoa, whoa, whoa-oh!*

Tom Jones must really like the word *whoa*.

I looked back to the girl named Rose, who was watching her hands as they traveled the keyboard. I turned to leave, but after a few steps I spun around for one more look, which caught her attention. I pointed at the floor and mouthed the words, "I'll be back tomorrow."

She gave me a quick thumbs-up before returning to the keys.

THREE

I MUST HAVE AN EFFECTIVE AUTOPILOT SETTING, BECAUSE I DON'T
remember the bike ride back across town to the café. My mind
was somewhere else the entire two-mile trip.

Somewhere involving a Tom Jones song-and-dance number.

Somewhere involving a World War II vet and the national
anthem.

But mostly somewhere involving a girl named Rose. And if
I timed it right, thanks to the 5-Day Deal, I'd get to see her for
the next four days in a row.

My delivery job had taken a sudden turn for the better.

That is, until I got the news.

The World Peas Café was located on the corner of Main
Street and the railroad tracks, in a run-down strip mall that also

featured a cash-loan place, a psychic, some kind of small-town detective agency, and Crazy Joe's Hot Slots. It was like one-stop shopping for people who would someday end up on *The Jerry Springer Show.*

Not that I ever watched that show . . . Crazy mom, remember? We grew up without a television. Mom believed in the power of imagination. Somehow I'd managed to grow up pretty normal—save for the occasional propensity to daydream—but my brother definitely took Mom's lesson to another level, which explained a lot about his compulsive mapmaking and battle planning.

The parking lot was nearly empty, as usual, except for a few beat-up cars, including our own. I was locking the bike to the light pole in front of the café when my mom started talking from the doorway. "Another cancellation of the 5-Day Deal, that makes two today."

"Cancellation?" I asked, stepping inside.

"I just got off the phone with the director of Hilltop Nursing Home. Apparently, the salad was 'overpriced and not what she was expecting,'" Mom said, adding peevish air quotes to the last part.

My heart sank. "Did you try to talk her out of it? What did you tell her?"

She threw her hands in the air. "I can't force people to eat my food, Zeus. If they want to live in a world of trans fats, hydrogenated oils, and factory-farm meat, that's their choice, but I can't change someone's free will."

I wanted to say: "*But, but, but* Hot Piano Girl!"

What came out instead: "That's bullshit!"

Mom crossed her arms and looked at me. "Watch the language, you. Care to rephrase that?"

"Um . . . *total* bullshit?"

Mom tried not to laugh and failed. "Complete and utter bullshit," she agreed. "But don't you dare say 'I told you so.'"

A rush of guilt hit me, and I looked down at my feet.

I'd fought tooth and nail for us to stay in Chicago. It's not like we'd lived some luxurious lifestyle there, but everything—my neighborhood, my school, our little house by the airport—had at least been familiar. Mom had busted her butt for years, though, and always for us. She'd never enjoyed waitressing, but she'd worked long hours so Grub and I could have food on the table every day.

She'd always dreamed of moving to a small town and opening a café, though I never thought she'd really do it. For one thing, she didn't have the kind of savings needed to start her own business. For another, I couldn't imagine her making us say good-bye to all our friends. But when the night came to sit us down and tell us it was actually happening, that my aunt Willow had loaned her the money to *make* it happen, I knew I'd lost the battle. I saw her excitement at the prospect of no longer serving eggs and bacon. I knew this was an opportunity for her to do something for herself and not just for us. I understood.

But that didn't mean I was thrilled about moving. And she knew it.

I looked back up at my mom. She wore a light blue T-shirt that read *We Are One* in a dozen different languages, blue jeans cuffed midcalf, and dollar-store flip-flops. Her brown hair was pulled back in a ponytail.

"I got a dollar tip," I said sheepishly, trying to change the subject.

"Well, that's a dollar more than you had before, isn't it?" chirped Mom, ever the optimist.

"So, how's the café doing, other than the cancellations?" I asked.

"Good," she said in a way that sounded like *Not good*. "I'm not throwing in the towel yet."

"To victory!" yelled Grub, raising a fist. He sat at one of two booths that occupied the café, drawing a map of the nursing-home battle he'd just fought.

"To victory indeed!" said Mom, walking over to him. She put her hands on his shoulders and looked down at the map. "Wow, that's quite the battle, Manny." (Mom refused to call my brother Grub; I refused to call him Manny. I guess in the end it all evened out.) "I recognize you there behind the plant, but who's in the wheelchair?"

"Sergeant Porter. He played army with me. I covered him when the enemy came out. I shot a rocket, but I missed the target."

"I see. And who's the enemy?"

"The mean lady."

"Missy Stouffer," I clarified. *"Overpriced and not what she was expecting,'"* I added, mimicking my mom's air quotes.

Mom stifled a laugh, which came out like a snort, then patted Grub on the shoulder. "Next time, don't miss."

And that's when I had the greatest idea that ever was, or ever shall be.

"Hey, what about your triple chocolate brownie?" I asked.

"Turn That Frownie Upside Brownie?" Mom replied.

I hated calling it by name. "Yeah, that one. What if we offered a free brownie and maybe a cup of soup to Missy Stouffer and the others who canceled? As a way to keep their business. What soup do you have this week?"

"Tomato bisque."

"No fancy name?"

"The only one I could think of was Life's a Bisque, and Then You Die."

"That doesn't sound very World Peas-y."

"How about I Say To*may*to, You Say To*mah*—"

"Yeah, *no*," I said, shaking my head at her. "So, free brownie and soup? I can deliver them to Hilltop tomorrow." I didn't have the slightest clue what I'd say to Rose once I got there, but I had to start somewhere, right?

She eyed me with suspicion again. "Why so eager to go back to a nursing home? You hated going when Grandma was sick."

"Yeah, that's because Grandma was *sick*. I love old people."

Mom narrowed her eyes.

"I love *you*, don't I?" I said, trying to make her laugh again.

"Good thing," she said, holding out her hand, "because I need to borrow your phone for a while."

I stared at her in horror. My phone, along with its instant access to social media, text messaging, and Google, contained my entire punk rock music collection. Without my playlists, I would never survive the summer.

"You're joking, right?"

"Just for a week or two. I dropped mine in the sink this morning, and I need a phone to take orders."

I thought fast. "But all the coupons and advertisements have *your* number on them, not mine. It won't work."

I felt like I'd won the battle until Mom delivered the death-blow. "I already chatted with the phone company this morning on the laptop. They forwarded my number to yours."

My shoulders slumped. I pulled my phone out. "Well, that would explain the four new voicemails from unknown numbers."

"Speaking of which, there are more deliveries to be made."

I loved my mom, but she needed a Nerf bazooka to the forehead right then.

"So I'm supposed to ride around all week without music?"

Mom showed no mercy. "Try listening to the birds, they're nature's music. You can have your phone back in the evenings." She handed me three more salad containers and a map of Buffalo Falls. "Sometimes you have to take one for the team, son."

I shook my head and handed over my phone.

It felt like I'd just ripped off my right arm.

"Now go be charming," she said, and pecked me on the cheek.

"Let's roll!" said Grub.

And so we rolled.

FOUR

OUR LAST DELIVERY OF THE DAY TOOK US ACROSS THE BRIDGE TO THE
south side of town. In fact, after fifteen minutes of uphill pedaling, we were nearly back at Hilltop. I tried to think of an
excuse to go back inside but couldn't find any good reason.
Soon we reached the delivery address, a trim brick ranch with
a sprawling maple tree shading the front lawn. Sweat dripped
from my face like big salty tears. I wiped my face with the
sleeve of my T-shirt, parked the bike on its kickstand, and
approached the house.

Grub planted himself on the lawn behind me, watching
the street for enemies. I walked past a picture window, its ledge
lined with a planter full of red geraniums.

I started to knock on the door when a sound left me frozen.

"Darling, don't be afraid, I have loved you for a thousand years..."

Whoever sat near the open window five feet from my head was belting out a love ballad.

"... I'll love you for a thousand more."

I stood there, unsure if I should let the guy finish the song or interrupt and knock.

My brother made the decision for me.

"Pew-pew! Pew-pew-pew!" Grub had rolled across the lawn and began firing his imaginary pistol at the window.

The singing stopped abruptly.

I knocked.

"It's open!" yelled the voice from the window.

Grub joined me at the door. I looked down at him and shrugged. He shrugged back. We let ourselves in the front door and stepped into a tiled entryway.

"Hello?" I said in a pitch much higher than intended.

The voice came from around the corner. "Yeah, back here."

Grub and I headed toward the sound of his voice. It led us through a short hallway, which ended with open doors on opposite sides. To the left, I caught a glimpse of a bathroom, to the right, a cluttered bedroom.

"Step into my office," said the voice in an odd way, as if it *were* an office.

I stepped inside and froze again when I recognized the

person. He recognized me too.

"Jesucristo!" the guy said, pointing at me.

"Shakira?" I replied.

"*Sí! ¿Cómo estás?*"

I tried to remember what little Spanish I'd learned in my one month at Buffalo Falls High School. "Uh, *muy bien.*"

"Haha, what's up, my man? Pull up a seat." He motioned to his bed. I sat. "You moved here from Chicago, right? You have a weird name in real life, don't tell me." He shut his eyes and tapped his forehead with his knuckles. "Hercules?"

"Zeus. Short for Jesús."

"Oh, right. Hence, *Jesucristo.*"

"*Sí.*"

Honestly, I was surprised he remembered me at all. I remembered *him*, of course. He was the kind of guy everyone noticed, the guy everyone wanted to be friends with. His real name was Dylan Rafferty, but Señora Stanford, our Spanish teacher, had nicknamed him Shakira, like the Latin pop star, due to his wavy, shoulder-length blond hair. And since another guy in the class had already been christened Jesús, she referred to me as Jesucristo, crossing herself Catholic-style every time she called on me. It'd been the only class I looked forward to, mostly because it was the last period of the day, but also because Señora was a wack job. The good kind of wack job though—the kind that randomly starts salsa dancing in the middle of class.

Dylan was the same age as me but looked about three years older. He leaned back in his desk chair, a tobacco-sunburst Gibson Les Paul guitar lying across his chest. His left leg was in a cast, propped on top of the desk. Long hair fell on either side of his face, the rest tied back in a messy knot. Thick sideburns extended to his jaw. From what little information I'd been able to gather during my time at BFHS, Dylan not only dated the hottest girl at school, but could also shred guitar. I wondered if the two things were related.

"Hey, *mi hermana* had to run," he said, forgetting the *h* was supposed to be silent in Spanish, "but she told me to pay for her *comero*."

I laughed. His Spanish was even worse than mine. "You mean her *comida*?"

"Her food-o deliverio," he said, twirling a finger at the salad box I held.

I laughed again. Dylan reminded me of the friends I'd left behind in Chicago: laid-back, funny, easy to talk to.

Just then, a giant beast of a dog entered the room and lumbered toward us. Its jowls hung like mud flaps, from which ropes of drool dangled an inch from the ground.

"Say hello, Agatha," Dylan said.

Agatha wagged her tail. Though her coat was light brown, she had a black face and ears to match. Grub walked up to her and they nearly met eye to eye.

"I bet she'd be a good bomb sniffer," Grub said, examining

the dog's huge nostrils.

"No doubt. She's an excellent *butt* sniffer." Dylan gave Agatha a playful slap on the hip. The dog leaned in and licked Grub's face from chin to forehead.

"Ohhhh, sorry about that, little dude," said Dylan, then turned to the dog. "A little less tongue next time, Aggs."

Grub giggled and wiped his face with his sleeve.

Agatha sat in front of him and held a paw in the air.

"Atta girl," Dylan said. "Now she wants to shake your hand, like a proper lady."

Grub stuck out his hand, which was smaller than her paw. "Nice to meet you, Agatha."

Agatha barked in agreement.

"So, what have we got here?" Dylan asked, eyeing the cardboard box I carried.

"Peas and Hominy."

"For sure. What's in the box?"

"That's what it's called."

"Oh, right on. How much?"

"Eight ninety-five."

Dylan reacted as anyone would after being told a salad named Peas and Hominy cost nearly nine dollars: a quick twitch of the eyebrows and mouth, followed by a head nod of justification.

We made the exchange, and Dylan opened the container

to inspect it. He made the same face as when I'd told him the price, then showed it to Agatha. She sneezed, shook her head, and flung drool around the room.

"It's actually really good," I said. "The peas are organic, locally grown, and—" I began, reciting Mom's delivery pitch.

He cut me off. "It's all good, man. Maybe I'll give it a try. Maggie—my sister—got called into work and won't be home till late. I could probably use a night off of deep-fried burritos anyway."

I nodded back. "Hard to beat a deep-fried burrito though."

"Hell yeah. So your mom owns that new place on Main Street? World Hunger Café or something?"

I nodded. "World *Peas* Café."

"She, like, a hippie-type?"

I shrugged my shoulders. "I guess."

Dylan chuckled. "She'd probably get along great with my parents. They're spending two months in India at some Buddhist retreat center. Just me and Maggie for now. And Agatha."

Agatha's tongue spilled from the side of her mouth as she smiled.

"Your parents left you guys alone for two months? That must be awesome."

It was Dylan's turn to shrug. "Kind of awesome. Maggie's a social worker, studying for her master's, so she's not around much. My girlfriend's away in Maine all summer, working as a camp counselor. And most of my friends have temp jobs at the moving company where I used to work before my little accident." He motioned to his cast-entombed leg.

I raised my eyebrows in question. "Little accident?"

Dylan blew out a breath. "Ladder. Squirrel. Life-and-death struggle."

"Sounds traumatic."

"Yeah, that squirrel was a real asshole." He set the salad box on his desk, then played a riff on his guitar. It was a simple slidey, bendy move, but much better than I could do.

A couple more guitars hung on his bedroom wall.

"How long have you been playing?" I asked.

"I guess about five years now."

"Cool. I've been playing for a few months, but I just have a shitty acoustic."

"You want to play one of mine? Here, let me—"

"No, that's okay. Thanks though. We have to get running. Maybe next time."

Dylan nodded. "Next time."

Grub was on his knees stroking Agatha's ears, relaxed in a way I hadn't seen him since we'd moved. I almost hated to interrupt him, but we'd been there long enough.

"Let's move, soldier, time to go."

"Do we have to? Look, she wants to play." Agatha had rolled onto her back, her big paws hanging limp over her chest. Agatha and Grub both looked at me awaiting an answer.

I patted Grub on top of his army helmet. "Not today, bud. Need to head back. Tell Agatha good-bye. Maybe we'll see her again soon."

"All right." Grub hopped up and darted out the door. "Bye, Agatha!" he called, his voice fading down the hall.

Agatha barked.

I started after Grub but something made me stop and turn back to Dylan. "By the way, was that you singing when we pulled up?"

Dylan's face turned as red as the Stratocaster hanging on his wall. "Uh, *that*, yeah." He held up his phone to show me. "My girlfriend, Anna, the one in Maine this summer? She loves Christina Perri."

"Right on," I said, unsure what that had to do with anything.

"Since I can't do much else, I spend most of my time playing guitar, recording shit to send her. Weekends me and my friends get together to jam down in the basement though. Thank God for that, or I'd totally be losing my mind."

"I bet," I said, looking at his guitars again. Part of me wished he'd ask me to jam with his friends. Another part was relieved when he didn't. "*Adiós*, Shakira. Hope that leg heals soon," I said, heading toward the door. I could hear Grub outside, shooting his bazooka.

"Amen, Jesucristo," said Dylan, crossing himself like Señora always did.

I scooped up Grub from the front yard, and we headed back to the café.

FIVE

BY THE TIME GRUB AND I GOT HOME, MY LEGS FELT LIKE RUBBER. MAK-
ing deliveries by car would have made a lot more sense, but
Mom's boxy red, stick-shift 1992 Ford Festiva had over a quarter-
million miles on it, and gas money was tight. So, the Lego—as
we'd somewhat affectionately nicknamed it—was only sanc-
tioned for top-priority excursions.

Besides, I drove stick shift about as well as I could pat my
head and rub my stomach at the same time. Which was to say, I
was crap at it.

I carried my bike up the five steps to the front door. Grub
covered me, watching the street as I unlocked the door and let
us in. Mom was still at the café, finishing up some paperwork
and cleaning.

Grub ran to his room.

"Hungry?" I called to him.

"Yeah!"

"Cheese bread or mac-n-cheese?"

"Mac-n-cheese!" he answered.

Interesting fact about Grub: he only ate foods that were white or yellow.

Or whitish.

Or yellowish.

That may sound limiting, but he found plenty to eat. Popcorn, corn on the cob—anything with corn, really—bananas, french fries, cereal, and cheese were the main staples of his diet. "He'll grow out of it," Mom always said.

I had my doubts.

That was one cool thing about my mom though—despite paving the vegetarian road to healthiness, she basically let us eat what we wanted.

After boiling up two boxes of mac-n-cheese, I plopped down on our fake leather couch in the living room, which doubled as my mom's bed. The apartment only had two small bedrooms, and she'd let Grub and me have them. In Chicago, I'd always had the basement bedroom, where I could blast my music as loud as I wanted and my friends and I could stay up late without bothering anyone. Now we could hear one another's slightest movements through the thin walls. But I tried not to complain.

I knew Mom had sacrificed a bedroom of her own to make the move easier on me and Grub. Me especially.

I picked up my guitar and strummed a few chords. It felt like a toy compared to the ones hanging on Dylan Rafferty's wall. For the past year I'd been wanting to get a black Fender Telecaster, like Joe Strummer's, the guitarist from the Clash. That hadn't happened, obviously. But three weeks before we moved from Chicago, Mom had walked in with an acoustic guitar she'd purchased at a garage sale. While it didn't compare to anything in Joe Strummer's—or even Dylan's—collection, it was pretty badass of her to get it for me. Mom knew I'd been wanting to learn guitar ever since I'd discovered *Combat Rock* in eighth grade.

I still dreamed of buying the Telecaster, but considering the way my delivery career was going, it didn't look like it would ever happen. I'd made a grand total of eight dollars and fifty cents in tips that day. At that rate, I could hardly afford to buy new strings for the guitar I already had.

I looked down at the sad piece of equipment. The old strings made my fingers smell like rust, and the few dead, pinchy noises I managed to squeeze from it were poor excuses for music, but still better than they used to be.

When I first got the guitar, I didn't know a single thing about it. For instance, no one warned me that pressing down on the metal strings hurt like hell. But after a couple days, calluses started forming on my fingertips. Then after a few more weeks of watching videos online, I learned three important skills: (1) how to tune it; (2) how to form a couple chords; and (3) the fastest way to retrieve your pick after it fell into the sound hole.

Three months later, I could play a halfway decent rendition of "I Wanna Be Sedated" by the Ramones. I'd read somewhere if I learned the G, C, D, and E minor chords I'd be able to play one thousand songs. Only nine hundred ninety-nine to go!

Just as I realized that a C chord could slide up two frets into a D chord, Grub came bounding around the corner and plopped next to me on the couch. He opened a cardboard box and began assembling Battleship pieces.

"Grub, not right now."

"One game," he pleaded, his brown eyes looking huge in his small head. Both Mom and I had trouble saying no to him, not necessarily because he was so tiny, but mostly because he was such a good egg, rarely complaining or asking for much.

I sighed. "One game." I set my guitar down, then placed my destroyer, submarine, cruiser, carrier, and battleship on the board. "All right, you go first."

"B-2," said Grub.

"Hit. So, fun time making deliveries today? A-9."

"Miss. Yeah! I finally made a new friend. C-2."

"Hit. You mean the old guy? F-7."

"Miss. Sergeant Porter. He played army with me. The kids

at my new school never played with me. D-2."

"Hit. They just don't know you yet. Give it some time. A-1."

"Miss. I don't think the kids here like the same things I do. E-2."

"Hit. What, no World War II buffs in second grade? G-10."

"Miss. No, they just talk about Pokémon and iPads and stuff. F-2."

"Maybe third grade will be better. Hey, you sunk my battleship!"

"I know, you always put it in the same place."

As we continued to play, I snuck peeks at my brother with equal parts affection and concern. Grub had handled the move to Buffalo Falls like a good soldier, dutiful and uncomplaining as always, but I knew Mom worried about him —and I did, too. The move had been hard enough for *me* and I was twice his age and relatively normal.

Both Grub and I had known our Chicago friends since we were in diapers. We'd never had to *make* friends; they were just always there, the neighborhood gang. We'd all roam from yard to yard, everyone's parents looking out after everyone's kids. When you grow up with people like that, maybe you accept them the way they are because you don't know anything different.

Grub was a fixture in our neighborhood, army helmet and all, and everyone loved him. He was just Grub to them. But here in Buffalo Falls, he was just . . . weird.

We finished the game without any more talk of Chicago or friends, sticking to easier topics like naval warfare. Grub won handily, of course, picking off my fleet like a German U-boat, then retreated to his room.

I was putting away the game when Mom burst through the door, dropped her purse, and hurtled off to the kitchen. "I've been thinking about it, and you're right, Zeus," she called. "We'll go ahead with the free brownie and soup tomorrow. We had another 5-Day Deal cancellation." From the kitchen I heard the *THOOP!* of a wine bottle opening, followed by a trickle.

"Really?" I was shocked she was using my idea. "That's awesome!" That meant going back to Hilltop Nursing Home tomorrow. Never in my life would I have considered that prospect exciting before now.

But this was different.

Rose would be there.

Rose.

Something about her felt . . . important. Special. *Something.*

Maybe it was the way she played piano. Or the way she looked. Or the way she looked at *me*. Whatever it was, I couldn't get her out of my head.

I picked up my guitar and strummed a few chords as I thought back to our encounter. When I told her I'd be back again tomorrow, she'd given me the thumbs-up. That was a good thing, right?

Or was it a sarcastic thumbs-up? What if she was just mocking me? She and her quarterback boyfriend were probably having a good laugh about it that very moment as they made out in the back of his Jeep Wrangler. That guy that threw his Slurpee at me? That was definitely him. Rose's boyfriend.

I pictured his hand sliding under her yellow sundress and felt like I might be sick.

I started scolding myself. *Stop it, Zeus. Why are you obsessing over her? God, you haven't even talked to her; why are you so worked up? Okay, so she's hot and she's awesome at piano. But you've talked to girls before; it's not like they're some foreign creatures. Chill.*

"How's the guitar coming along?"

Mom appeared before me out of thin air, snapping me out of my neurotic daydream. "I suck."

"Language, son. Let me ask again—how's the guitar coming along?"

I sighed. "I'm grossly underdeveloped in my musical competence, but I'm showing slight signs of improvement."

"There, see how much better that feels?"

It didn't feel better, but it didn't feel worse either. "I ran into two kids my age today who are somehow both incredible musicians. How is that possible in this backwater?"

"Maybe this backwater's good for creativity."

"Or maybe there's nothing to do here but practice."

Mom joined me on the couch. "So tell me more about your new friends."

"I wouldn't call them friends. More like customers. The guy was in my Spanish class and plays guitar. The girl plays piano at the nursing home. And I'm sure they both have a ton of friends already."

"And *I'm* sure they've got room for one more." Mom gently slapped my leg. "Especially one as delightful as you."

"Yeah, right," I said, rolling my eyes. "Everyone around here has been friends since kindergarten. They're not interested in making new ones."

"Oh, nonsense." She faced me and tucked one leg beneath her, a knowing grin on her face. "So tell me more about the girl."

My face immediately turned the color of her wine. "What about her?"

"You like her, do you not?" she asked, eyeing me from behind her glass. "I'm your mother, remember? I know when my son's hormones are raging."

"Mo-om," I said, drawing out the word into two syllables, the universal shorthand for "If you don't stop talking, I will cut off my ears with a steak knife."

She rolled her eyes at me this time. "Okay, okay. No need to get cranky. You certainly won't make new friends that way."

And then all of sudden I *was* cranky. "Seriously, do you have any idea how humiliating it is to ride around on a woman's bike, with your crazy little brother clinging to your back shouting army crap the whole time? Do you really think I'm going to make new friends *that* way? Some guy even threw his drink at us earlier."

Mom winced. "I know it hasn't been easy, but—"

"Not to mention I can't even text my Chicago friends now. They probably think I'm dead."

"But you said you made some new friends today."

"Are you even listening?"

Mom set her glass down and put a hand on my leg. "Zeus, I'm sorry about your phone, but we all have to make sacrifices sometimes."

"How many do I have to make?" I asked, my voice rising. "You moved us to the armpit of America where I have no friends and nothing to do. I ride a dumb bike, work for nothing but tip money, and keep Grub entertained for you. And now you take my phone? Why can't you just buy a new one?"

Mom blinked and looked away, then got up and walked to the door where she'd dropped her purse when she came in. She pulled out the phone and handed it to me. "I'll need it back in the morning," she said, still not looking at me. "I don't have money for a new one right now, Zeus." I could tell she was trying not to cry.

"Mom," I said, but she was already walking to the kitchen.

That night as I lay in bed, I listened to "Kiss Off" by Violent

Femmes on full volume through my earbuds. *I need someone, a person to talk to. Someone who'd care to love. Could it be you?* Tomorrow I'd try to figure out the chords on my guitar, but right then all I wanted to do was feel the music inside me like a wave.

It was angry.

It was frustrated.

It was lonely.

As I drifted off to sleep, I wondered what Rose would think of it.

SIX

THE NEXT DAY I SPED THROUGH MY DELIVERIES IN RECORD TIME. IT WAS nearing two thirty, so I hoped Rose would still be at Hilltop playing piano. I careened down the sidewalk while Grub held tight. We had returned with the tomato bisque and brownie, hoping to win back Missy Stouffer's business. Well, *that* plus an additional objective, which is why I'd packed an extra brownie.

"At attention, soldier!" Sergeant Porter shouted as we approached. The same nurse from yesterday stood behind him, pushing him through the nursing home grounds.

"Sergeant Porter!" said Grub, jumping off the bike pegs and running toward the old man.

"I'll need a debriefing on any new intel you've gathered by fifteen hundred hours."

"Sir, yes, sir!"

"As you were."

What may have been a smile quivered across the old man's face; it was hard to tell. His advanced age had given him a permanent scowl.

Grub unstrapped his Nerf bazooka and took up position behind some shrubbery near Sergeant Porter, who nodded at him in approval. Every now and then Grub would make a run for another bush at the old man's command.

The nurse and I stood in silence for a moment, watching the unlikely pair guard Hilltop from imaginary foes.

I finally cleared my throat and turned to her. She had the same dark features and coppery skin as Rose, only the nurse was a little shorter and plumper. Her eyes looked tired, but her face was kind. "Ma'am, I hope you don't mind my brother. He's a little different."

She held up a hand. "Don't even think of it. He's the first person Blackjack has connected to in weeks," she said, glancing at her charge. I followed her gaze.

The man saw us looking at him and yelled. "Why don't you bunk lizards stop yapping and give us a hand!"

"Blackjack, *kumalma ka*," she called.

"*Ako ay kalmado,*" Blackjack muttered loudly.

"What does that mean?" I asked.

"I told him to relax, and he told me he *is* relaxed. I grew up in the Philippines, where he was stationed during the war, so we share a few phrases. It's amazing, really. He has almost perfect retention of the Tagalog words he learned seventy-some years ago. And then some days he forgets who I am."

"Alzheimer's?"

She nodded.

"Is it bad?"

She smiled and gave a slight shrug. "He has good days and bad days. But he recognized your little brother right away, which is great."

I thought back to Grandma and shivered, even though the day was hot. She'd had Alzheimer's and I'd hated it, watching her become someone I didn't recognize—someone who didn't recognize *me*. I'd missed her before she was even dead, mourning the person she used to be, the Grandma who always knew how to make everyone feel loved and special.

"What's your brother's name?" the nurse asked, breaking through the memory.

"Manuel, but my mom calls him Manny. I call him Grub."

"And what does he call himself?"

"*Private* Grub," I said, raising my eyebrows.

She laughed, and I noticed she had the same smile as Rose. "Of course." She waved at Grub and gave him a salute, then turned back to me. "I'm Mary Santos. That's Sergeant John Porter, but everyone calls him Blackjack."

"Nice to meet you, Mary. I'm Zeus."

"Nice to meet you, Zeus. Making another delivery?" she asked, nodding to the cooler in the bike basket.

"Sort of. I guess the director didn't like the salad yesterday, so it's more of a complimentary kind of thing."

"I see. Well, I believe Ms. Stouffer is in the common room with some of the residents, if you want to head in."

"Great— Uh, will there be music today?"

"Every weekday from one to three," she said with the same knowing look my own mom had given me last night.

I shifted uncomfortably until Blackjack saved me.

"Get me out of this jungle, I'm sweating my balls off!" he bellowed.

"Panoorin ang iyong wika!" Mary scolded, going over to retrieve him.

I didn't know what that meant, but I imagined it had to do with him talking about his balls. I followed them back to the arched entryway, and much like the day before, Grub crawled, rolled, and dove ahead of us. As we entered the building, a wave of Lysol hit my nose again.

That was going to take some getting used to.

The same woman sat behind the reception desk, but she must have recognized us from the day before because she waved us in and returned to what she was doing. As we continued down the hall, I could hear the piano. My heart skipped a beat and I felt a quick rush of adrenaline. As we got closer, I noticed the music had a much different tone compared to the Tom Jones dance party yesterday. It was nostalgic and sad and hopeful all at the same time.

When the end of the hallway opened into the common area, I saw the mood of the music had permeated the room like a haze. No one danced, no one sang. Hell, no one even stood, except for Missy Stouffer, who walked around writing on a clipboard. Everyone else had been hypnotized by the piano's soaring, wistful notes, lifting them far away from Hilltop Nursing Home. I looked over to Rose at the piano, expecting her to wink, or smile, or somehow make me blush, but she looked straight down at the keys, fully immersed in the music. It was beautiful.

She was beautiful.

I could have stood there and listened to Rose play all day, but Missy spotted me like a hawk on a field mouse. It took her a moment, but when she recognized me, she held her hands out and shook her head quickly, her body language saying, "What do you want? Can't you see I'm busy?" I held up the box containing the soup and brownie. She repeated the same motion as before, even more exaggerated this time.

Screw it, I thought, and started walking over to her. Realizing she was going to have to deal with me, she approached me as well. We met at the edge of the seating area.

She spoke in a loud whisper. "What are you doing here? I

specifically canceled my order yesterday."

I matched her loud whisper. "Yes, you did. We're just offering a complimentary cup of tomato bisque soup and a triple chocolate brownie as a way to say thanks for your business."

Her eyes narrowed as she peered at me over her red frames. "Triple chocolate brownie?" she asked, attempting to hide her interest.

"It's made with all-natural ingredients. The chocolate is imported from—"

She cut me off, grabbing the box from my hands. "I'll take it. Thank you." She spun back into the common room and hissed at Rose. "Play something cheerful, you're upsetting the residents."

I looked over to Rose, who hadn't noticed I was there yet. She smiled tightly, then transitioned straight into "If You're Happy and You Know It" without missing a note. Missy tried rousing the crowd by singing the words and acting them out, only to be met by a few off-timed claps, thuds, and groans.

"Why don't *we* get special deliveries? The food here tastes like horseshit!" yelled the Tom Jones Cackling Woman from yesterday. The two old ladies beside her grumbled in agreement.

Missy whipped around on her heel. "Letty Kowalczyk, if you don't watch your language, you'll need to stay in your room during activity time."

"Oh, go on!" called Letty. "You know this place would be duller than a pig's ass without me!"

Missy took a deep breath and turned to one of the nurses on duty. "Please remind Mrs. Kowalczyk that her profanity upsets the residents and is inappropriate in group settings." She clipped away toward her office, opening the cardboard box as she went.

"Of course, Ms. Stouffer," said the nurse, though Ms. Stouffer was already well out of hearing range by then.

Letty glanced at her two sidekicks and rolled her eyes.

By the look of things in the room now, Rose was on the "if you're happy and you know it, fall asleep" verse. I checked the clock. Almost three o'clock on the dot. Rose would be finishing soon. That meant—what? Run up to her, drop the box on the ground, and run away? No way. Loser move. I'd have to say something first. "My name is Zeus. I've brought you a brownie." No, too formal. "I've been watching you play. I brought you a brownie." That made me sound like a stalker. "Hey, what's up? My name's Zeus." Perfect. Then go for the handshake and compliment her playing. Solid plan. Smooth as silk. Anything after that would be a bonus.

Now was my chance.

I checked Grub's status. He'd hidden behind the potted plant as soon as he'd seen Missy. Good. He could hunker down there for now.

I'm not going to lie—my heart was pounding out of my chest at that point. Rose finished the song and one of the nurses addressed the residents, telling them music time was over. The ones that could stood and shuffled past me, while others were wheeled away.

And then, it was just the three of us in the room. I was only ten feet away from the piano. Rose pulled the sliding black cover over the keys, then walked toward me.

I held out the box. "It's a brownie."

What? There's no way I told my mouth to say that. My first words ever spoken to her could not seriously have been "It's a brownie." *Plan failed, abort mission! Escape! Seek cover!*

"Thanks," she said, taking the box. "Are you okay?"

I must have looked a mess. "I'm lovely. Uh, I'm great . . . you're love . . . you're welcome." What language had just come spilling out of my mouth? *Dear God. Please get me the hell out of here. Love, Zeus.*

"Okay, well, good-bye," I said, then turned to walk away, hoping to find the nearest hole to crawl into.

"Wait."

I turned around. "Me?"

She smiled and stuck out her hand. "I'm Rose."

My hand met hers. "Zeus." Her skin was soft and warm.

"So did you make the brownie?" she asked, nodding to the box in her other hand.

I finally released her grip and shoved my hands in my pockets. "Yes. No. Sort of."

I sounded ridiculous.

She raised her eyebrows at me.

I babbled on. "Let's just say I made the brownie happen. That's all I'm allowed to tell you. The rest is a matter of national brownie security."

She laughed. *Thank God she laughed.* "How mysterious. Thank you."

Relief washed over me like a tidal wave. I think I started breathing again. "No problem. I hope you like it."

"I'm sure I will. So you work at that new café on Main Street?" she asked, looking at the sticker on the box.

"Yeah, my mom owns it. You should check it out some time."

She leaned toward me as if to whisper in my ear. "If I do, will I get a glimpse of the secret brownie operation?"

She was close enough I could smell her perfume, or lotion, or whatever girls wore. I stopped breathing again.

"Absolutely. Better go now," I said, pointing to the exit with my thumb over my shoulder. "Work to do. Back at the café."

She smiled, then walked past me in an aromatic whoosh of sun-ripened raspberries and vanilla. "I'll stop in soon. See you, Zeus."

"See you, Rose."

Yes.

SEVEN

I WASN'T SURPRISED WHEN ROSE DIDN'T MAKE AN APPEARANCE AT the café that same day. I'd expected that, even though I stuck around later than usual, just in case. No big deal. Giving her at least twenty-four hours seemed perfectly reasonable. If I were her, I'd wait a day too.

Wednesday arrived, bringing with it another day of deliveries. Adding to my general level of humiliation and discomfort, Mother Nature showed up for work an emotional wreck. Periods of bright, intense sunshine alternated with thunderous downpours, as if she were having delusions of grandeur one moment and sobbing about it the next. By the end of the day, Grub and I looked like sewer rats, our hair and clothes drenched with rain and sweat.

Wednesday afternoon, still no Rose. Nor had Missy Stouffer called to place a new delivery order. But no need to panic. It was still midweek. I'd give Rose another day before I lost all hope.

Thursday was a cloudless, Rose-less, hundred-degree day. From the minute we walked out the door, the humidity hovered at steam room levels. I sweated a gallon for every mile I pedaled. I tried to convince Grub to stay behind in the air-conditioned café, but he insisted the heat didn't bother him, that it was fun.

And still no Rose. Despite all my best efforts, my natural defense mechanisms began to kick in. I felt like I was back in psychology class learning about the stages of grief.

Denial. She's still coming. She *had* said, "I'll stop in soon," right? Yes. If not today, then definitely tomorrow. Nothing to worry about.

Anger. Definitely not coming. So why did she say she would? Just to toy with me? I hope I never see her again.

Bargaining. Maybe she's busy. Maybe something happened to her. I shouldn't have hoped I'd never see her again.

Depression. I've made a complete fool of myself. What made me think she'd ever come?

Acceptance. Well, it was fun while it lasted. At least I got a handshake out of it.

By Friday, I had convinced myself that I shouldn't spend any more time obsessing about Rose. Thank God Missy Stouffer had canceled her salad plan and I'd never have to go to Hilltop again. Instead Grub and I made our usual deliveries downtown with no risk of running into anyone I'd later waste hours and hours thinking about. It was probably a good thing too, since the temperature remained in the triple digits, causing me to sweat through a new T-shirt every hour. I remembered being little, playing in the sun all day and barely breaking a sweat. Now I rode my bike one city block and my armpits turned into faucets. What the hell?

We finished our deliveries and returned to the café to turn in the money. Grub jumped off the pegs and covered me as I parked the bike on its kickstand and approached the door with the money bag.

"All clear, sir!"

"Thank you, private."

My mom darted around the café watering the numerous hanging plants. Big shocker—Mom was a plant fanatic. I grew up learning all the Latin names of her houseplants. My favorites were spider plants (*Chlorophytum comosum),* snake plants (*Sansevieria trifasciata),* and the pothos (*Epipremnum aureum*). When I was younger, she'd grab a wooden spoon from the kitchen and shout the Latin names at me—*Hedera helix!*—as if casting spells in *Harry Potter.*

It might sound kind of lame but I used to love it.

"Mom, whatever all-natural, goofy deodorant you buy me isn't cutting it. My pits are sweating like Niagara Falls and I smell like a dog fart." I set the money bag on the counter, then leaned on it with my elbows.

Mom turned to me, then motioned with her head. "Someone's here to see you." I looked in the direction of her nod, and a cold sweat rushed down my spine when I saw who it was.

Rose sat at a booth and gave a shy wave. "Hi," she said.

I froze as my brain attempted to decode the situation. A moment passed, then another, though it felt like hours.

Say something! said part of my brain.

Do something! said a different part.

I wiped the sweat from my forehead with my sleeve, then smiled and waved back, still leaning on the counter. "Hi," I replied.

Nailed it.

"BZSHOO!" Grub lay prone on the floor, Nerf gun aimed straight at Rose.

Rose feigned a wound, grabbing her chest with both hands. "You got me!" She slid down the booth, a casualty of café warfare.

"Grub, don't—" I began.

Rose popped her head back up, laughing. "It's okay." Then she turned to Grub. "But watch out! Next time I'm bringing my grenade launcher."

"Manny, come give me a hand," said Mom from the back of the café.

"On my way!" yelled Grub, crawling away on his stomach and elbows.

And then we were alone, me a sweaty mess still leaning on the counter, Rose looking like a ray of sunshine. I tried to think of something funny or clever or cool to say, but the image of me bursting through the door babbling about my personal-hygiene issues replayed through my mind. I held a long blink to erase it.

"How's it going?" I finally asked. "I didn't expect to see you here."

"Yeah, sorry I couldn't make it sooner. I didn't realize the café closed at four. I usually don't leave Hilltop until five."

I waved it off with a flick of my wrist. "No big deal," I lied. "Glad you made it." That much was true. "Mom just serves breakfast and lunch here for now. I should've told you."

"It's a really nice place." Rose looked around, nodding her head in approval as if seeing it for the first time.

"Were you—have you been here long?" I stammered.

Rose shrugged her shoulders. "Not really. I've been hanging out with your mom. She's awesome."

"She's pretty cool," I agreed, eyeing the kitchen door, wondering if Mom could hear us.

I took a few steps toward the booth, unsure of what to do next. I hadn't thought this through. Just minutes ago I'd convinced myself Rose didn't exist. Now, here she was. This was what I'd wanted, right? For her to show up at the café?

"Yep." I paused, glancing at the parking lot. "Cool if we take your car?"

Rose paused too, and bit her lip. "I don't have a car. I walked here."

"No problem." *Plan B it is*, I thought. "Hold tight just a second." I stuck my head in the kitchen where Mom and Grub were washing dishes and lowered my voice. "Hey Mom, can I borrow the Lego? Just for a couple hours?"

"Sorry, the Lego is reserved for *friends* only, not customers."

Ouch. She clearly hadn't forgotten my less-than-civil proclamation the other night that I'd never make friends here. "Please?"

She turned to face me with a smug mom look, then grabbed the car keys from her purse and tossed them to me. "Just be home before dark."

"Thank you." I whirled out of the kitchen and joined Rose near the front counter. "All good," I said, jangling the keys.

We walked back outside, where the humidity hovered between Amazon rainforest levels and the inside of a mouth. I walked to the passenger door first and unlocked it for Rose.

Grub came running out of the café. "I'll ride bazooka!"

"Wait! Grub!" I said, trying to grab him, but he'd already pulled the passenger seat forward to climb in back.

"Ride bazooka?" Rose repeated, looking amused.

"It's what Grub calls riding in the back seat of the car, or on the back pegs of my bike. You know, instead of riding shotgun in the front. Riding bazooka."

Rose looked at Grub, who'd taken up position in the rear, guarding us from enemy attack. "That's really cute," she said.

"Yeah," I said, unconvinced. How the hell was I going to get Grub out of there without looking like a jerk?

Mom appeared in the nick of time.

"Come on, Manny, I need you to stay here and guard the café," she said, leaning into the car. "We can make banana bread."

Grub whipped his head at Mom, then hopped out of the Lego. "Yes!"

"And here *you* go," said Mom, handing me a full thermos and a baggie of homemade trail mix. "In case you two get hungry."

"Thanks, Mom," I said, holding her gaze a second longer to let her know I really meant it.

"Sure thing. Have fun!" she called, herding Grub back into the café.

"Let's try this again," I said, holding the passenger door open for Rose.

"What a gentleman," she teased. I shut the door behind her, then walked around to the driver's side and let myself in.

Next came the fun part: driving that fucker.

It had been a while since I'd last driven, months ago, in fact, when I'd borrowed our neighbor's car in Chicago to make a food run.

And it hadn't been a stick shift.

"You can drive stick shift?" asked Rose as I strapped on my seat belt. Despite the windows being down, the inside of the car was surface-of-the-sun hot, and the vinyl seats blistered the back of my legs.

"Yeah, I got this." I replied. I was fairly certain the clutch had something to do with starting the car.

"You just push the clutch in," I began.

I pushed the clutch in.

". . . turn the key,"

I turned the key.

". . . and give it a little gas."

The engine turned over, I floored it, released the clutch, and screamed as the car backfired and shut off.

Rose clapped a hand over her mouth, unsuccessfully trying to suppress her laughter.

I laughed too, which made her laugh more, which made me laugh more, which turned into an all-out laughing fit. She actually had tears in her eyes and hiccups by the time we were done. After a few more attempts, I got the Lego running, and we headed off to Metea State Park, wherever that was.

EIGHT

"MIKINAK OVERHANG," ROSE READ OFF A SIGN AS WE WALKED FROM the asphalt parking lot onto the hiking trail.

"I wonder what that is?" I replied.

Rose shrugged. "I guess we'll find out."

"So you've never been here either?"

"Nope."

"When we aren't back by Christmas, they'll send search parties, right?"

Rose laughed. "We won't get lost, look." A map of the park lay just ahead on a brown metal stand, cemented to the ground. Plexiglas covered the map, upon which people had etched proclamations of eternal love, *For a good time call so-and-so*, and a number of rudimentary phalluses.

"You are here," I said, pointing to the respective balloon-shaped arrow on the map.

Rose turned her head toward me. "See? We aren't lost. We're *here.*"

I laughed. "Glad that's settled. Okay then, onward?"

"After you." Rose gestured for me to lead the way, then joined me on the trail.

The drive there had been a comedy of errors, but after several wrong turns, a couple engine stalls, and one bifurcated raccoon carcass, we'd found the entrance to Metea State Park. It should have been simple—a ten-mile straight shot west on Route 17—which I'd have known if I'd had the map app on my phone. Instead, I decided to follow the Stone River, cruising ten miles per hour under the speed limit, unable to find fourth gear. An hour later, totally lost, I admitted my blunder and Rose navigated us the rest of the way on her own phone.

Aside from the rhythmic murmur of the cicadas and our footsteps, we walked in silence. After a few minutes, Rose spoke. "Those were some pretty sweet driving skills," she teased.

"You know, my sarcasm detector isn't broken," I teased back.

A laugh escaped her lips. "Seriously, you did great. When I took drivers' ed, I flunked the driving part of it. Like, the important part, where you have to *drive.*"

"Really?"

"Oh yeah. A very proud moment. I'm pretty sure I ran over

every orange cone, drove through a red light, and when I parallel parked, we were five feet from the curb. Traffic was backed up for three blocks."

"If it makes you feel any better, I still can't parallel park."

"Oh, I'm a pro now," Rose responded. "I could parallel park a bus."

I looked at her and smiled. "I'd like to see that." My awkwardness percentage had dropped to around eighty after lingering near a hundred since she'd shown up at the café. "So you share a car with your mom too, huh?" I asked.

"I guess, if you can call it that. She still freaks out about me driving."

"Maybe it had to do with flunking drivers' ed?" I joked.

She shook her head and laughed. "Shut up. No, she just worries. It's only the two of us, so sometimes I think I'm all she has to worry about."

I almost asked about her dad, but decided she'd offer that information when she was ready. Besides, I didn't like talking much about mine. "How long have you been playing at Hilltop?" I asked instead, lifting a small branch that had grown over the trail for her to walk under.

"I started last summer, then worked a bit over Christmas and spring break, and now again this summer. My mom's been working in the memory care unit since we moved to Buffalo Falls three years ago, so she was able to get me the job. I don't make much money, but I get to play the grand piano."

"You're really great, Rose. I'm sure people tell you that all the time, but it's true."

"Aw, thanks. I love it. It's probably my favorite thing to do."

"I can see why."

The trail led us deeper into the woods. It began as compact dirt, but soon became sand the color of bone. In contrast to the prairie and cornfields surrounding Buffalo Falls, the park had a mystic, definitely not Illinois feel. Large green ferns unfolded below ancient oaks and maples. Red-headed woodpeckers flitted from tree to tree, jackhammering their faces into the bark in search of food. The odd chipmunk scampered across our path, stopping on hind legs to look guiltily at us, then scurry away.

After a half hour or so, we came upon a wooden bridge where we took a moment to rest, appreciating the cool breeze brought by the rushing water of the creek below.

"This place is amazing," I said. "I can't believe it's only a fifteen-minute drive from town."

"*Should be* a fifteen-minute drive."

"We happened to take the scenic route today. We should come back in the fall, when the leaves turn."

Rose didn't reply, just stared at the water. I noticed she had a dimple on the left side of her mouth, above her chin. The late afternoon sunlight danced through the leaves, illuminating her face with broken light.

I wasn't sure if she'd heard me, so I repeated myself. "Wouldn't it look awesome here in the fall?"

After a pause, she flashed a quick smile at me. "For sure. Come on, let's keep going."

Ahead, a stone staircase had been carved into a towering hill. As we climbed, the air seemed to cool a degree with every step—a welcome relief. The stairs, spaced several feet apart, created an unusual climbing rhythm: UP, step, step, step, UP, step, step, step.

Halfway there, we saw the payoff at the summit: a giant sandstone cave burrowed deep into the cliff. At least a hundred feet high, the gaping cavern looked big enough to bunk an army platoon. Grub would have loved it. We craned our necks to take it all in.

"Wow," Rose said. "This is incredible."

By the time we finally reached the mouth of the cave my thighs were burning, but it was worth it. Rose and I began to explore different ends of the cave. The ground was hard and covered with trampled dead leaves. Charred remains of campfires spotted the perimeter, the occasional half-incinerated beer can decorating the ash. The soft sandstone walls were a time capsule—fresh carvings jumped out, sharp edged and deep, while older ones had been smoothed by the years.

"Hey, look at this!" called Rose. She now stood in the center of the cave, under the rim. Her head was tilted back and her tongue stuck out. I walked over to meet her and looked up as well. White roots hung far above, dripping cold water.

"Are you sure you should drink that? It's probably . . ."

"Probably what?" she asked, tongue still out, making it sound more like "Mammahly mah?"

"I don't know, like deer piss, or something. Aren't you not supposed to drink random cave water?"

She lowered her head and looked at me with raised eyebrows, as if I'd just told her I'd seen a unicorn in the trees. "If I die, please tell my family I loved them, and that I died as I lived, drinking questionable cave water." She stared at me straight-faced for a moment, then burst into laughter. I laughed too.

"All right, all right. It can't be worse than my mom's agave lemonade," I said, setting the thermos on the ground. I joined her under the dripping roots and tilted my head back. The first drop splashed off my forehead. The second, my right eye. The third hit the side of my mouth. By the fourth, I had the target locked.

Direct hit to the back of the throat.

I choked.

"There's sand in it!" I hawked at the back of my throat, like when a popcorn shell lodges there.

"Really? No sand in mine. You chose poorly," said Rose, leaning her head back to catch more.

I must have been feeling brave then because I approached

Rose to playfully push her out of the way for a better claim on the nonsandy-water drip. A simple-enough plan in theory, yes, but where it went awry was upon execution, due to an uninvited, unannounced, and generally unpleasant arrival of a third party.

A brown spider the size of a quarter had somehow planted itself upon Rose's left breast. After a brief moment of jealousy, I reacted as any sane person would under the circumstances.

"Whoa!" I proclaimed, pointing directly at Rose's chest.

Rose, head still tilted back, raised an eyebrow. "Seriously?"

"Spider!" I finally spit out. Rose looked down, her eyes widening as she spotted it. I think it waved back.

She screamed and swatted it at me.

I screamed and spun like a matador dodging a bull.

I'm sure the spider was the most scared of all, and have no doubt it screamed too as it cartwheeled past me into the leaves.

I brushed myself off, performing a top-to-bottom inspection. Rose did the same.

"What a perv. That spider totally just made it to second base," I said.

"No kidding. It didn't even buy me dinner first."

I paused for a moment. "So what are your dinner plans tonight?"

She slapped my shoulder. "Shut up! I just got fondled by a spider. I need to start saving for therapy."

"*You?* I just pulled some *Matrix* shit. I'll need a chiropractor."

A laugh fell from her mouth. "You're funny."

I knew it was my turn to say something, but suddenly I forgot every word I'd ever learned. I just looked at her as a warmth spread from my chest to my fingertips all the way down to my toes. She looked back.

I softly cleared my throat. "Well, then."

Rose smiled and bit her lip. "Well, then."

She walked under the dripping roots and tilted her head back again.

I joined her.

Turns out cave water tastes delicious after all.

NINE

WE SOON DISCOVERED A TRAIL LEADING OUT THE OTHER SIDE OF THE cave, descending deep into the lowlands of the park. Once at the bottom, the cool funk of mud, decay, and oxygen-rich air filled our nostrils. We traipsed through hidden channels and canyons—green, moss covered, and hauntingly beautiful. Stray beams of sunlight penetrated the canopy, illuminating tiny moths, which fluttered among the foliage. We traveled a narrow path along a creek that buckled and gushed around stray timber. The source of the flow soon revealed itself in the form of a seventy-foot waterfall.

It felt like we were in a movie.

Almost.

Before the waterfall stood a family of six, arranged by height and decked out in matching outfits in complementary colors.

The dad, fumbling with a camera on a tripod, waved us over enthusiastically. "Hey guys, mind doing me a huge favor?" he asked with a salesman's toothy smile.

Normally it drove me nuts when people asked me to commit to a favor before revealing what said favor was. Mom was the queen of that. And *huge* favors were the worst, because people would deceive you with smaller, no-big-deal favors first, then pounce on you unexpectedly, like a hungry puma. Before you can blink, you're mucking out a flooded basement or babysitting your neighbors' tyrant offspring. Like so:

Mom: Will you do me a huge favor?

Me: Sure.

Mom: Take out the trash?

Me: No problem.

Mom: Will you do me a huge favor?

Me: Sure.

Mom: Put that tofu back in the fridge?

Me: No problem.

Mom: Will you do me a huge favor?

Me: Sure.

Mom: Leave Chicago behind, move to a small town, and start a new high school one month before final exams?

Me: . . .

But in this case, I knew exactly what "huge favor" the man wanted, so I decided to comply.

"Sure, we'll take a picture," I said as the youngest in his brood broke formation.

"Thanks, bro," he said, as if he were sixteen too, not forty-seven. "Just press that button there. Take a bunch, don't be afraid."

"Got it," I replied.

"Don't be afraid, Zeus," Rose whispered once the man was out of hearing distance.

"I'll try, but don't leave me, just in case."

"Don't worry, I'm here for you."

The man hustled back while barking out orders. "Maisie and Marlo, switch places with each other. Michael, straighten your shoulders. Honey, grab Mason before he shoves more sand in his diaper. All right, gang, everyone look natural!"

"Everybody say 'jalapeño-cheddar-jack cheese!'" said Rose.

After I snapped a dozen of what felt like the exact same picture, the man thanked us again, then he and his wife herded their litter away.

"They better send us a Christmas card," Rose said, then pointed left of the waterfall, where large sandstone boulders studded the hill. "Let's go sit over there."

We climbed to one of the flatter stones that looked like it could seat both of us. I attempted to brush the sand from it, which proved to be as easy as brushing water from a puddle. We sat anyway.

"You said you moved here three years ago. Where from?" I asked.

"Iowa City. My dad taught history at the University of Iowa, but now he's up in Minnesota."

"I've never been to Iowa City. Do you miss it?"

"A ton. It's a cool town, really artsy. Lots of music and festivals. It has this beautiful outdoor Ped Mall where they have the Iowa Arts Festival. Jazz bands, craft shows, food trucks . . . I used to go every summer when I lived there."

"I know how you feel. There was so much to do in Chicago. I'm not sure if I'll ever get used to this town." I kicked a loose piece of sandstone and watched it tumble into the water below.

"How long ago did you move here?" Rose asked.

"April."

"Gotcha. I guess that's why I don't remember seeing you at school."

We sat for a while watching the water crash off the rocks. The static noise covered our own silence. I remembered the bag of trail mix Mom had packed and pulled it out of my pocket. The chocolate morsels had long ago melted, coating the nuts and dried fruit with a sticky layer of confection.

"Want some?" I offered the bag to her.

"Absolutely."

"So, how long have you been playing piano?" I asked. "You must have started before you could walk."

"Not that long ago, actually." Rose licked some melted

chocolate from her knuckle. "A little over three years, right when I moved here."

"What?! How's that possible? You don't even use sheet music."

"I know it sounds crazy, but piano just makes sense to me somehow. I mean, think about it. It goes from left to right, low to high. Twelve notes and they just keep repeating. Black keys are sharps and flats, white keys are naturals. They all fit perfectly together."

I snorted. "For *you* maybe."

"I suppose. For some reason my fingers just seem to know where to go. Do you play anything?"

I hesitated. "I have a guitar."

"That's awesome!"

"I've only been learning for a few months. I wouldn't call it *playing*, but I can make a few noises come out of it," I admitted.

"Sweet, you'll have to show me sometime! I've never played a guitar, but it can't be that much different from a piano, can it?" She looked out into the crashing water. "It's all just notes, whether it's a voice, or a piano, or a guitar, or a tuba. Vibrations. Harmony and dissonance. Major and minor. Check it out— hear that hum from the waterfall? *Mmmmmm*," she hummed. "Hear that?"

I listened. It sounded like water to me. "Uh, I don't think so."

"It's there. *Mmmmmm.* I bet I could find that note if I had a piano here. Music is everywhere. My music teacher told me she once had a student with perfect pitch. He could listen to the second hand on a clock ticking and tell you what note it was."

"That's nuts." I listened again for the hum of the waterfall, but still couldn't hear it. I believed her though. "So what are your plans this summer? Besides playing at the nursing home?"

"Well, I'm usually at Hilltop noon to five, Monday through Friday. I play the piano and help out with whatever else Candy, the activity director, wants me to do. I got out a little early today so I could stop by," she added, her cheeks turning the slightest bit pink.

"Cool," I said, trying to look casually pleased though I was, in fact, absurdly pleased.

Rose continued. "Then on Saturdays my mom drives me up to Naperville, where I have my lessons. My instructor's teaching me music theory and how to actually *read* music. I just taught myself by ear until a year ago."

"By ear? That's amazing, Rose. I noticed you didn't use sheet music when I was at Hilltop. So someone shouts out Tom Jones, or whatever, and you can just play it?"

"Usually, as long as I've heard it before."

I shook my head. "That's crazy."

"Well, the Hilltoppers do tend to request the same songs over and over again. But I try to play some of my own favorites, too, for a little variety."

"That first afternoon I walked into Hilltop, you were playing this song. . . . The melody's been stuck in my head all week."

"Hum it for me."

I hesitated, then tentatively began to *hmmm-mmm* my way through a few bars of the song.

Rose grinned and nodded in recognition. "*That* one."

"So what is it? I know I've heard it before. It's driving me crazy."

"Not telling," Rose teased.

"Is it by the Beatles?"

"Maybe."

"Deep cut?"

"Maybe."

I laughed. "Okay, okay. It'll come to me eventually."

"I'll wait," Rose said, grinning again.

"You better. So what came before your piano rock-star status? Test pilot? Child ninja?"

"Ha, I wish. I've gone through some phases, I guess, but just the usual. I had my video-game phase, my dance phase, my drawing phase. I don't know. Nothing seemed to stick until piano. What about you? What's your story?"

And for the next hour we talked. I learned she'd be a senior this year; she learned I'd be a junior. I learned her parents had divorced when she was ten; she learned I'd never met my dad. We talked about Chicago and the universe and the Beatles and my weird plant knowledge. For a while we sat silent and let the sound of the water do the talking for us. I couldn't believe how well everything was going. Eventually, our conversation circled around to future plans.

"What comes next?" I asked. "You'll be a senior, so does that mean college in a year?"

Before Rose could answer, the sound of distant chatter floated toward us, quickly turning into the unmistakable roar of screaming children. They descended upon our sanctuary like locusts, at least fifty of them, mud covered and wet. It must have been some sort of summer-camp outing, based on the small number of frazzled twenty-something-year-old chaperones trying to maintain control. The buzzing swarm flew past us up the sandy hill, claiming the land as their own. Rose and I shared a look, shrugged our shoulders, and laughed.

Before long, the horde left, but by then the sun had started to set and our once sunny spot had been overtaken by the growing shadows of the cliff wall. Since the park closed at dusk, we headed back to the car.

As I drove back to town, the sun at our backs and the windows down, I looked over to Rose, whose hair flew wildly in the wind. She stared out her window watching the trees and houses whip by. A low fog had settled over a bean field. Ahead, a half-full moon rose, glowing orange and crimson, mirroring the sunset. When we arrived back in town, the streetlights had turned on, giving the world a luminescent glow.

I'd never felt happier sitting next to someone.

Yes.

Maybe.

Pretty sure.

Oh, hell no.

Most definitely.

Now what?

I took a quick survey of my surroundings. Mom would be closing soon to clean and prepare for the next day. Not a cool place to hang out if I wanted to be alone with Rose, which I did. "Do you want to go somewhere?" I asked, nervously shuffling some pamphlets on the counter.

"Sure! I'm up for whatever. Where do you want to go?"

My mind went blank. If we'd been in Chicago, I'd have had a hundred ideas. But Buffalo Falls? Where the hell was there to hang out? Under the bridge? My eyes fell upon the pamphlet in my hand, titled *Top 10 Hikes at Metea State Park.*

"Hiking?" I said, surprising myself at the sound of the word. I'd never been hiking in my life. In fact, I had no idea where Metea State Park even was. Where I grew up, hiking meant taking the Orange Line train downtown to Navy Pier. And how would we get to the park anyway—with Rose on the back pegs of the Schwinn? Or worse, take the Lego?

"That sounds fun," Rose exclaimed, her eyes lighting up.

Damn. This wasn't going to end well at all.

Rose popped up. "Ready?"

TEN

THE FOLLOWING AFTERNOON, A SATURDAY, I STOOD ON DYLAN RAF-ferty's doorstep again, salad in hand. A young woman opened the door, his sister, Maggie, no doubt. They shared the same wavy blond hair and chestnut eyes. She held a phone to one ear.

"Hold on a sec," she said into the phone, then to me, "You must be Zeus, the salad guy. Come on in, just give me a minute to wrap this up."

I walked into the living room, where Dylan sat on the couch with his guitar. He wore a Foo Fighters T-shirt and cargo shorts, showing off one tan calf, the other white as snow.

"Hey, Shakira, you got your cast off!" I said, pointing to the paler limb.

"*Esta mañana*, my man," he replied, motioning to an

armchair nearby. "Have a seat."

"Gracias." I plopped the Save the Kales salad on the coffee table and sank into the chair, grateful for the air-conditioned reprieve.

"Where's your little sidekick?" Dylan asked. Agatha, who sat at his feet, lifted her head and barked, as if she also wanted to know.

"Grub? Slow day, so my mom let him stay behind at the café. Sorry, Agatha."

The dog laid her head back down.

Dylan stretched his newly liberated leg. "So how was your Friday night?" he asked. "Do anything fun?"

"Actually, it was pretty great," I replied.

"Awesome! What'd you do?"

I hesitated before answering, unsure if it would, in fact, sound "pretty great" or "awesome." "So there's this girl, Rose, who plays piano at the nursing home—"

"The Filipino girl? Piano prodigy?"

"Yeah, you know her?"

Dylan shrugged. "Just by sight. I've never had a class with her, but I've seen her at school. She's the quiet type. I hear she's got some serious talent though."

"She does," I agreed.

"Go on."

"Right. So I met her at Hilltop on a delivery last week and

asked her to stop by the café sometime. She doesn't show up for days, then all of a sudden she shows up yesterday."

"Out of nowhere." Dylan made a *poof* motion with his hands.

"Yep. So we ended up heading out to Metea State Park to hike. But I've never hiked in my life. And I had to drive my mom's little stick-shift car from the nineties. Not to mention I was sweaty from making deliveries all day."

"Rough start."

"Tell me about it. But it ended up going great. She's really cool. We sat by this waterfall talking for like an hour."

"Nice. That's awesome, man." Dylan played a quick bluesy riff, then folded his hands across the guitar and leaned in toward me. "So, what do you like about her?"

It's funny, because as much as I'd thought about Rose since we'd first met, I wasn't really sure how to answer him. I liked a lot about her, of course. Her smile, the dimple below her lip, the way her hair blew in the breeze, her insane musical talent. The way she didn't seem to mind all the things that went wrong. She made me feel like I could be myself. She made me want to be with her. But I didn't exactly feel comfortable telling any of that to Dylan, someone I barely knew.

"I don't know," I muttered. "There's just something..."

"In the way she moves?"

"No, it's something—"

"In the way she knows?"

I looked up at Dylan and finally caught the joke. He held a closed fist over his mouth to keep from laughing.

"Ha! You like the Beatles?" I asked Dylan.

"Who doesn't?" he replied, strumming a few chords from "Something." It reminded me of my conversation with Rose.

Then again, everything reminded me of Rose now.

Maggie bustled back into the living room then, sliding her phone into the pocket of her jeans.

"Thanks for waiting," she said, handing me some cash. "Hey, D, my friend Angie has two extra wristbands for Buffalo-Fest tonight. You want them?"

"Hell yeah," said Dylan. "I've hardly left the house in weeks."

"BuffaloFest?" I asked. "Is that the carnival down by the river?"

"Every summer!" Dylan replied. "It's an institution around here."

"Sounds fun," I said, though I wasn't so sure.

"It's awful," confessed Maggie. "But an awesome kind of awful. You guys should go!"

An uncomfortable pause followed. Maggie had just put us both on the spot, but Dylan especially—as if he didn't have a hundred friends he'd rather go with. I opened my mouth wordlessly, but Dylan recovered first.

"Yeah, man, we should go," Dylan said. "Meet you there at eight?"

"Sounds like a plan."

* * *

Dylan and I walked down the carnival's main causeway, occasionally stepping over black electric wires that snaked their way across one another to power iffy-looking rides. We took turns renaming them: the Barf-a-Whirl, the Not-So-Funhouse, the Humper Cars, Ali Baba's Death Machine . . . you get the picture. The aroma of corn dogs, asphalt, and body odor saturated the stagnant June air.

Every few minutes, we'd stop so Dylan could catch up with someone he knew. It didn't take long to realize why he was so well liked—the dude was nice to everyone. And I mean *everyone*. Including me. Every time we got stopped, Dylan introduced me as "Zeus from Chicago" and explained that I was new to town. A few kids remembered me from school, but most of them didn't. I stopped trying to keep track of names after it became clear Dylan knew half the population of Buffalo Falls.

Before long, twelve of us stood near the Gravitron. Dylan's group of friends had a favorite summer tradition—seeing who could survive the ride without regurgitating a corn dog or deep-fried Twinkie. Once they found out I'd never been on such a contraption, the friendly chatter turned to urgent persuasion.

"Dude, it's like a ritual. You have to come with us," said a guy named Joe or maybe John but definitely not Justin.

"No, I'm good, thanks. The guy operating it looks like an escaped prisoner," I replied, "not to mention he's lit like a bonfire."

"Come on, Zeus! It's a rite of passage in Buffalo Falls," urged a girl who I think was Katie, but may have been Jenny. "I'm sure this ride has a four-star safety rating."

"Out of what, a hundred? No, you guys go ahead. I've already met my vomit quota this month."

I tried backing away from the group, but Dylan put his hand on my shoulder. He looked me in the eyes, smiled, and nodded to the ride. "You're coming with us."

As I flashed my wristband to the attendant, I advised the group that I wasn't responsible for my stomach contents ending upon or near them. We boarded the spaceship of death and took our spots.

If you're like me and unfamiliar with the Gravitron, allow me to explain. Basically, it's a UFO-shaped unit with lots of flashing lights. Inside, the walls are lined with vinyl pads from floor to ceiling. A bearded man in cut-off jean shorts sits in the center working levers and switches like the Great and Powerful Oz. Once the whole operation starts spinning, centrifugal force sticks everyone to the wall like bugs smashed on a windshield.

I couldn't wait.

I'm kidding.

I could have gone to my grave without ever experiencing the Gravitron's pleasures, but peer pressure's a beast.

We took our places and waited for the ride to start. Then, slowly, we spun. When the lights began to blur through the opening in the ceiling, I shut my eyes. I felt my brain get sucked to the back of my skull as the speed increased. At its top velocity, the floor dropped out, a scenario that I was neither warned about nor prepared for. A sound escaped from my throat, much like a dog makes while getting his tail stepped on. I braced for the inevitable equipment malfunction. But when I opened my eyes, I was still firmly cemented in place by the laws of physics. We spun for another minute, like a flying saucer about to launch. Finally, the ride slowed down, my stomach returned to its normal resting place, and we all stumbled from the Gravitron in varying degrees of vertigo.

"See, man? It's not that bad. And you didn't even hurl!" said Dylan.

I swallowed the extra saliva that had pooled in my mouth, still fighting the urge to puke. I held my thumb and index finger together in an okay sign.

Dylan turned to the group. "We'll catch up with you guys later. I've got a few more initiation rites in store for Zeus."

For a split second, I imagined myself being wheeled out of BuffaloFest on a stretcher. We said our good-byes as the group headed off toward a ride called the Freefall, which looked like it had been pieced together with chicken wire and paper clips.

"All right, now let's get you a funnel cake," said Dylan. While my stomach wasn't fully on board with the decision, I played along. He led me a short distance to a neon-colored hut, brightly lit from within by fluorescent tubing. Dylan ordered our food, and then we continued to walk as we ate. After a while, he looked at me with a powdered-sugar mustache. "Verdict?"

Despite my initial reluctance, I'd devoured half the tower of powdered-sugar-covered dough like a starved hound. "I think I just got diabetes," I replied.

"I told you it's good," he said, inhaling another mouthful. We were polishing off the last few bites when Dylan's phone dinged and interrupted our feast. He licked the sugar from his fingers and pulled it out. A smile crept across his face, illuminated blue from the screen. "Check it out," he said, turning it toward me. A brunette, blue-eyed beauty wearing a tank top and pajama bottoms looked back at me making a pouty face. The text said *MISS YOU* followed by six exclamation points.

"Your girlfriend?" I asked, though I was pretty certain.

"Mm-hmm. Anna. We send a picture every night before bed. It's almost ten o'clock East Coast time, so it'll be lights-out for her soon."

"Oh yeah, she's in Maine, right? Camp counselor?"

"Yep. Camp Harakawa." Dylan posed with a big bite of funnel cake in his mouth, then flashed a selfie and sent it to Anna. "She'll like that one," he said. His phone dinged again and he snorted as he read the text. "Anna wants me to win her a stuffed animal. What is it with girls and stuffed animals?"

For a fleeting second, I thought about Carrots, the stuffed rabbit I slept with until I was five. Okay, maybe six. Six and a half. Mom still kept him in a shoe box wrapped in tissue paper, even though he'd lost an ear, a cottontail, and most of his fur during his years of loyal service. Good old Carrots.

"No idea," I said.

"Me neither. All right, let's go lose some money! I think I saw some stuffed owls back there."

"Anna like owls or something?"

Dylan shrugged. "She loves the *Harry Potter* movies. I think there's owls involved."

"Chlorophytum comosum," I mumbled to myself.

"What's that?"

"Nothing."

We continued on through the flashing lights, buzzing alarms, and screeching sirens. As we passed two guys trying their might at a speed-bag game, my breath caught in my throat as I spotted a tan girl with black, wavy hair watching them. My eyes lit up, and I lifted my hand to wave but pretended to slick my hair back instead when she turned and I realized it wasn't Rose.

Luckily Dylan hadn't noticed. He stood with his arms crossed, facing a tent, frowning. A vinyl banner read: *TAKE HOME A GOLDFISH!*

I stood next to Dylan. "What's up?" I asked.

"You know, the fact that this still exists is a complete travesty."

I watched as a young girl tossed Ping-Pong balls into bowls of colored water. They all missed, bouncing off the rims. "You mean how all these games are rigged?"

"Oh, they're definitely rigged, a travesty in itself. But I'm talking about the goldfish, my friend."

Just then, the young girl sank a ball into a bowl and squealed. Moments later, out came her prize. The attendant handed her a clear plastic sack of water containing her new pet goldfish.

Dylan continued. "Ten years ago, man. It was traumatizing."

"What happened?"

Dylan shook his head at the memory. "I'd completely mastered the arc. One after another, boom, boom, boom, sinking them like LeBron James. I won seven goldfish that night. *Seven.* I was the happiest kid at BuffaloFest. I named them after the seven dwarfs. But what I didn't realize at the age of six was that fish need a certain amount of oxygen to survive. Oxygen they aren't going to get in a plastic bag. So that night they swam in their aquatic hourglasses, the minutes ticking away until their deaths."

"Didn't your parents tell you to put them in a bowl?"

"Yeah, well, my sister was babysitting me that night and she was too busy messaging her boyfriend to give me the requisite goldfish survival tips. So come morning poor Dopey was belly-up. Next went Happy, who was obviously *unhappy*, flapping himself in a circle with one gill on the surface. By lunchtime Sleepy was dead as a doornail, *not* sleeping, as I initially thought. Then Grumpy's eyes glossed over, Bashful sank to the bottom, and Doc developed a weird twitch before succumbing to Death's cold grasp himself. That night, Goldie was the last to go, having watched all six of his friends go before him."

"Wait, *Goldie*? I thought the seventh dwarf was Sneezy?"

"Fish don't sneeze, dude."

"Good point."

Dylan rubbed his chin and shook his head, staring at the goldfish game. "Why some animal rights coalition hasn't shut this operation down still baffles me."

I pictured my mom standing vigil in front of the booth holding a sign that said *GOLDFISH ARE PEOPLE TOO*. I put a hand on Dylan's shoulder. "It's okay, man. I'm sure they're in a better place now, with fishbowls the size of Nebraska and unlimited fish flakes."

Dylan sighed. "I hope so. All right, onward. I have a prize to win."

For the next half hour, we tried our luck at the ring toss, whack-a-mole, and milk jugs, only to walk away empty-handed. We considered entering the rubber ducky race, but decided we were a decade too old for that. Finally, after making nineteen points in sixty seconds at a basketball shootout game, Dylan was the proud new owner of a four-foot-tall stuffed giraffe.

"Perfect," he said, shoving it under one arm. "All right, dude. One more thing we have to do before we leave."

"After you," I said.

ELEVEN

I FOLLOWED DYLAN AS HE CUT BETWEEN TENTS, LEADING US TO THE far edge of the carnival. Beyond the Ferris wheel and bumper cars lay a row of food tents. Grill smoke hovered above us. The smell of cooked meat made my mouth water instantly, despite having eaten a pound of deep-fried sugar earlier.

"Had to give you the traditional carnival fare first, but this is where the real food's at," said Dylan, forging ahead.

As we neared the tents, I could make out some of the names: *Bobo's Gyros*, *Billy Bob's BBQ*, *Wang Chung Cantonese*, *Papi's Tenderloins*, and *Arduini's World Famous Pizza*. Dylan insisted I'd have to try all of them at some point—apparently they were as integral to Buffalo Falls's infrastructure as the roads and bridges—but tonight, pizza from Arduini's would suffice.

As we walked up, I said, "You'll have to understand my skepticism about the 'world famous' part. I *am* from the pizza capital of the nation."

Dylan grinned. "You'll thank me later."

At the counter, a girl our age stood smiling, her light brown hair framing her face. "Hey, Dylan! How've you been?" she asked.

"I'm good, I'm good. Finally walking again."

A sympathetic look flashed across her face. "Oh, I heard about that. Your leg all better now?"

Dylan shrugged. "Ninety percent. Getting there. Kaylee, this is Zeus." He threw his arm around my shoulder and presented me. "His family just moved here from Chicago."

She looked at me a moment. Then her eyes widened and she pointed at me in recognition. "World history? Mr. Donahue? Second period?"

I dug through my memory but didn't recognize her. "Uh, yeah. Did we meet?"

She laughed. "No! You were scary. We thought you hated us."

My stomach sank. "Really?"

She laughed again. I could tell she laughed a lot, but not in a ditzy way. "No, I'm totally joking! I just remember you sitting there, not talking to anyone. But I'm sure it was weird for you, being the new guy thrown in at the end of the year."

"Yeah, it was a little weird," I lied. It had been more than weird.

"Well, maybe we'll have another class together next year!"

I smiled. She had a cute sprinkling of freckles across her nose. "I promise not to look like I hate everyone if we do."

"Deal!" She turned back to Dylan. "How's Anna doing? I see her post all the time about how much fun she's having. It looks amazing out there!"

"She's doing great! I just won her this handsome fellow," he said, holding up the stuffed giraffe.

"Awesome! You two are so cute together."

Dylan pulled the giraffe to his cheek and stroked its head. "Aw, thanks. We try. He doesn't say much—his head is full of stuffing, after all, and he can't speak—but he's a very good listener."

Kaylee laughed some more. "Stop! I meant you and Anna."

As Dylan joked around with Kaylee, I watched him in admiration and not a small amount of envy. He was so easygoing with everyone, so comfortable in his own skin. I could learn a lot from him. *God,* I couldn't believe I gave off the impression I hated everyone at my new school. I'd have to work on that.

"Nice meeting you, Zeus!" chirped Kaylee, handing us each two slices of pizza.

"You too, Kaylee!" I answered, trying to match her exuberance.

"See you around, Kay," Dylan said, then turned to me. "Let's grab a table over there."

Rows of green picnic tables sat under a white canopy. White lights crisscrossed overhead like electric cobwebs. About half the tables were occupied, and I recognized a few faces from our Gravitron experience. I thought we'd join the group, but Dylan chose an unoccupied table in the corner. We sat next to each other, the giraffe across from us. Despite still feeling a bit ill from the funnel cake, I managed to shove both pieces of Arduini's World Famous sausage, onion, and mushroom pizza down my gullet in record time. And Dylan was right—it rivaled some of the best slices I'd had in Chicago.

"So, Kaylee's pretty cute, huh?" said Dylan.

"Yeah, definitely."

"She's single, you know. *Recently* single. I'm thinking you may be the perfect rebound material for her."

My hesitation said it all. "Yeah."

Dylan understood immediately. "Oh, I get it. Rose."

I nodded.

"Right on. I didn't know you two were serious."

"Well, it's still early. But so far, so good."

"Did you make plans to see her again?" Dylan spun himself around with his back resting on the table and crossed his legs on the bench across from us. I did the same.

"She said to stop by the nursing home sometime this week,

so I thought I'd drop in Monday after my deliveries."

Dylan whipped his head at me. "Monday? Oh no, no, no. You gotta wait until Wednesday. Tuesday at the absolute earliest."

"Seriously?"

"Dude, think about it. Remember how you told me you waited around for her all week, then she didn't show up until Friday?"

"Yeah, but she has a job. She was working."

Dylan gave me a look. "Point is, if you go rushing in to see her first thing Monday, you'll look desperate. Give it a day. Let her wonder if you're going to show up. Trust me."

"That sounds kind of, I don't know . . . manipulative."

"I prefer to call it strategy. Trying to understand girls is like trying to predict the weather, but I've learned a thing or two."

He was probably right. I mean, he actually *had* a girlfriend. "All right, I guess I can wait until Tuesday."

"You'll thank me later. So, what's your plan? You going to bring her something? Ask her on a date?"

"My *plan*?" I pictured myself riding Mom's bike across town with a stuffed giraffe on the foot pegs. *Bad plan.* Maybe I could bring Rose one of Mom's homemade, gluten-free Rice Krispie treats? *Better plan.*

"Yeah, your plan. Or are you just going to walk in there, throw your arm around her, and ride off into the sunset?"

Well, something like that, I thought. "I was thinking I'd bring her something from the café."

"All right, all right, that's a start. Listen, girls like confidence. But don't be *too* confident, just sure of yourself."

"Confident but not *too* confident," I repeated.

"Right. Take the lead. Show her you've been thinking about her without saying it."

"Take the lead."

"Think of it like guitar. If we're both playing a solo at the same time, it's like we're stepping on each other's toes, in the way."

I nodded. He didn't need to know I couldn't play a solo.

Dylan continued. "On the other hand, if we're both just strumming chords, playing rhythm, nothing much is happening. It's boring. We're both waiting for the other to do something."

"Waiting to do something," I said, still nodding my head.

"Right. So when you walk in there, what's the plan?"

I thought hard for a moment. "Um, not play rhythm?"

Dylan waved his hands in the air as if erasing an invisible chalkboard, then gave me a friendly pat on the shoulder. "You know what, don't even worry about it. I'm talking out of my ass. You got this. Go in there, say something nice, and ask her out."

"Say something nice, ask her out," I repeated. I knew it wasn't Dylan's fault, but suddenly I was completely freaked out at the prospect of seeing Rose again. Ask her out *where*? What the hell would I do with her in Buffalo Falls—hang out at a nursing home? I needed to gather more information. "You lived here your whole life, right?"

"Yessir, born and bred."

"How long have you and Anna been dating?"

"I guess about two years? I mean, I kissed her in fifth grade, but I don't think that counts. Yeah, I'd say we've officially been dating for two years."

"Sounds serious."

"Yeah, pretty much." Dylan explained how he and Anna planned on going to Buffalo Falls Community College together after graduation, then attending the University of Illinois to finish out their degrees. Anna wanted to go into education and become a PE teacher, Dylan wanted to pursue engineering, with a minor in music.

"Cool. So what do you and Anna do for fun around here?"

"Oh, you know, we hang out in each other's basements playing video games, watch TV, do homework together. The usual."

"I don't have a TV *or* a basement. I guess I'm screwed, huh?"

"Nah, man. It sounds like Rose likes you. You're golden."

I sighed and looked at the flashing carnival lights. In Chicago, there'd have been all kinds of things to do with Rose—North Avenue Beach, Navy Pier, the Riverwalk—free entertainment!

Of course, I'd never had a girlfriend in Chicago, but Dylan

didn't need to know that. Sure, I'd hung out with plenty of girls in the neighborhood, but they'd practically felt like sisters or cousins, I'd known them so long. I guess the closest I'd ever come to having a girlfriend was going to the frosh-soph mixer with Abbie Shoemaker last year. We'd texted for a few weeks before and after the dance, and actually had a pretty good time while there. But it soon faded away to nothing and she moved on to someone else for the next dance.

I slowly blew air through my cheeks. "I just don't know how to move forward with Rose." I paused and turned to Dylan. "I'm open to suggestions."

Dylan thought for a minute, then clapped his hands together. "Hey! What about this—your mom owns a restaurant, right?"

"Well, it's a café."

"But it has a kitchen?"

"Yeah . . ."

"You should offer to cook for her. A little romantic, private, after-hours dining."

My stomachache returned at the thought of asking Rose on a dinner date. What if she said no? Worse, what if she said yes? The only things I'd ever cooked were mac-n-cheese, frozen pizza, and popcorn, and I'd even screwed them up a time or two.

I imagined the conversation: "Hi, it's me, Zeus. From the hike. I was wondering if you'd like to join me for pepperoni pizza tonight? No, not delivery, frozen. We can have some pudding cups for dessert. Oh, you're busy? Me too. Sorry to interrupt. Good-bye."

Dylan must have noticed the blood leave my face. "Whoa, not trying to freak you out or anything, dude. But you have to be a little creative around here. It's not Chicago."

"I think that's an understatement."

"Trust me. Dinner. She'll love it."

Before we left, Dylan and I shook hands, or at least it ended up that way. It began by him offering a fist pound, me shaking it, then him correcting to a handshake and me fist-pounding his fingertips. After our impromptu secret handshake ended, we parted ways, agreeing to hang out again soon. All in all, it had been quite the successful weekend.

Now I just had to make it until Tuesday.

TWELVE

tory. Tuesday finally came, and I approached Hilltop carrying one of Mom's gluten-free Rice Krispie treats. Dylan's advice had been running through my head like a mantra: *Say something nice, ask her out. Dinner. She'll love it.* I'd been watching You-Tube videos on my phone the past couple nights and felt like I could at least boil water and butter bread.

I parked the bike and walked with Grub through the automatic doors. As I'd hoped, beautiful piano music drifted from the common room. I didn't recognize the song, but I recognized the girl. I'd heard the phrase "my heart skipped a beat" before, but never understood it until now.

I tried to give myself a quick pep talk. After all, we'd had a great time together hiking, right? So why was my heart racing?

Out of excitement? And if so, why did excitement feel so much like absolute terror?

Approximately twenty residents sat around the piano on various lounge chairs and sofas. Letty, the ringleader, sat cross-legged on a couch. Blackjack remained in his wheelchair at the perimeter with Mary Santos.

"Let's go, private," I said to Grub.

We walked up to Blackjack and Mary, who had their backs to us. When we were close enough, I cleared my throat. "Excuse me, Mrs. Santos?"

She turned, and her eyes lit up when she saw us. "Hi, Private Grub! Hi, Zeus!" she said in a loud whisper, motioning for us to join them. She put a hand on my shoulder, pulling me in. "I heard you and Rose had a fun time on Friday."

She told her mom it was fun. Score! A tiny bit of confidence returned.

"It was. Hopefully we can go back there sometime."

"I'm sure she'd like that. And you don't have to call me Mrs. Santos. Mary is fine." I nodded as she continued. "I'm so glad you brought this little soldier with you," she said, motioning to Grub. "Blackjack has been asking about him." She gently shook the old man's shoulder. "Blackjack, look who's here."

Blackjack turned, nine decades of bone, sinew, and muscle working together to slowly move his huge frame around. His eyes fell fiercely upon me, his mouth a thin, lipless line, sagging in the corners. But then his eyes lowered to Grub, and recognition sparked.

Grub lifted a hand to his brow in salute.

The corners of Blackjack's mouth twitched, almost a smile. He raised a feeble hand to his brow, returning the salute. "I thought we'd lost you."

Grub approached him and stood at attention. "We've had reports of enemies in the hallways."

Blackjack straightened his back, as much as he could, then looked at Mary. "The private and I will secure the perimeter. We'll report back at fifteen hundred hours with any intel."

Mary squinted her eyes and nodded at the unlikely pair. "I'd better join you two—in case you need extra backup." Mary turned to me and winked. "I think I see a seat open on the couch, by Letty. Rose will be done in five minutes or so."

I looked at Letty, remembering her foul mouth and dance moves.

"She's harmless, I assure you. Sometimes she can be a little shocking, but she's a real sweetheart."

Still, I eyed the seat with suspicion.

Mary patted my shoulder. "Don't worry, she'll love you." She wheeled Blackjack away, and Grub trotted along behind.

I looked at the spot on the couch next to Letty, then at Rose, who hadn't seen me yet.

Here we go, I thought. I'd wait until Rose finished playing, then: *Say something nice, ask her out.*

As I wove through the crowd, several confused heads turned to look at me.

I waved.

One waved back, another blinked. The third, Letty—dressed to impress in a flowery nightgown, pink slippers, and hair curlers—grinned and slapped a bony hand on the cushion next to her.

I sat two cushions away.

She scooched over. "What's your name, kiddo?"

"Uhh . . . Zeus."

"Gesundheit!" she said, then raised her voice to a holler. "Someone turn down the AC. It's like a goddamn morgue in here! Not all of us are dead yet, you know."

All heads turned to us then, including Rose's. I felt my face heat to extra warm.

Rose bit her lip and gave me a little wave.

I smiled sheepishly and waved back.

"So what'd you say your name was, kid?"

"Zeus Gunderson," I said, enunciating clearly this time.

"Letty Kowalczyk," she countered, sticking out a hand, which I shook. She patted her hair curlers. "Usually I don't let handsome young men see me like this, but I just got out of my spa treatment."

"Spa treatment?"

"Oh, sure! Second Tuesday of every month."

"It looks nice," I said, unsure how to respond.

"The gals and I like to get all dolled up, don't we?" She waved over two plump women, also in curlers, sliding by on yellow-tennis-ball-clad walkers. "Hey Bettys," Letty called. "Come meet my new pal, Zeus. Don't shake his hand though. He has a cold!"

The women propelled themselves across the shiny floor like beginning ice skaters, their slippered feet never leaving the ground.

"This here is Betty," Letty explained to me, pointing. "And this here is the other Betty."

I nodded as if I understood.

"Oooh, you got yourself a young'un'!" said Betty.

"Younger than the last!" said the other Betty.

"I like 'em young," said Letty. "That way they can keep up with me!"

Letty winked at me to let me know she was joking, but it felt like my face was on fire, verging on extra crispy. I held the box containing the Rice Krispie treat in a death grip.

Rose peeked over her shoulder again at the commotion. "Oh my God!" she mouthed, grinning.

"Save me!" I mouthed back.

Rose quickly finished the song and headed over.

The Bettys had launched themselves closer, trapping me against the couch. As I pondered the odds of successfully squeezing between them, their eyes raised to the distance.

"Aw, shit!" said one.

"Fun's over," said the other.

Letty leaned in close and whispered, "Follow my lead, kiddo." She lifted a leg and rested her foot on my knee. Her nightgown fell away, exposing a pale, skinny leg.

The nursing home director, Missy Stouffer, appeared, clipboard in hand, red-rimmed glasses perched at the end of her nose. She looked at me with eyebrows raised, waiting for an explanation.

"Do you have a visitor's badge?" she asked with an "I'm not messing around" look.

"He's not a visitor, he's my personal volunteer. Isn't that right?" Letty said, looking at me. I nodded back, confused. "He's rubbing my bunions. Helps with the swelling." Letty tilted her head at me, then to her foot, then back at me. I formed a pincer with my thumb and forefinger, removed her pink slipper, and started rubbing. I looked at Ms. Stouffer and nodded.

"Volunteer," I spat, unsure of what I'd just committed myself to, but hoping it'd be over soon.

Mary had reappeared behind Ms. Stouffer, along with Grub and Blackjack and a perky-looking woman with bright red hair whose name tag read Candy.

"That's right, Ms. Stouffer," said Mary, putting a hand on Grub's shoulder. "And this little soldier has been volunteering with Mr. Porter, whose short-term memory has been improving after his visits."

"You're goddamned right," Blackjack said, glaring at Ms. Stouffer.

Ms. Stouffer cleared her throat and pushed up her glasses. "I see." Then she turned to the redheaded woman. "Candy, as volunteer coordinator, I expect you have their paperwork in order?"

"I'll have it on your desk first thing tomorrow," Candy said, looking at me and smiling broadly, though her eyes said "don't even think about leaving here without filling out those papers."

I nodded back, suddenly understanding I'd just been volunteered for more than an afternoon. *Crap.* The last thing I'd planned on doing this summer was becoming a nursing home bunion rubber. I wondered if it was too late to change my mind, but then Rose caught my attention. She smiled and nodded eagerly, mouthing the words "Do it!"

And that was that.

"Count us in," I said to Missy.

"Well then," said Missy, looking at me and Grub. "Welcome to the Hilltop community. We appreciate your service," she added thinly, then marched off to her office, clipboard clasped to her chest.

"Thanks," I said to Candy and Mary, who still stood behind me. I looked over at Letty. "You too," I added.

"Sure thing." She wiggled her foot. "Who told you to stop rubbing?"

I rubbed.

"Hey there," Rose said, biting back a smile as she joined the rest of us by the couch.

"Hey there," I said back. I worked at Letty's bunion with one hand and held the Rice Krispie treat in the other, while everyone watched. I felt like a confused zoo monkey with a crowd of field trip students pointing and watching as I did monkey things.

"This is for you," I said, holding out the box to Rose.

"Thanks, kiddo!" said Letty, grabbing it. "The food here tastes like horseshit."

THIRTEEN

DUE TO MY NEW VOLUNTEER STATUS AT HILLTOP, i NOW HAD AN EXCUSE to see Rose every weekday after finishing my deliveries. And Dylan's sister, Maggie, had ordered the 5-Day Deal, asking to be the last delivery of the day to accommodate her work schedule. So each afternoon at two, Grub and I would stop by Dylan's before heading to Hilltop.

Though newly mobile, Dylan hadn't been authorized by his doctor to return to work at the moving company, so he seemed to appreciate our daily visits. The feeling was mutual all around, and the visits lasted longer each time. While Dylan and I talked music, guitar, and girls, Grub played in the backyard with Agatha.

As for Hilltop and Rose, I still hadn't worked up the nerve to ask her to dinner. Admittedly, the nursing home common room wasn't exactly the ideal location to have a private conversation. Mostly I'd just steal glances at Rose while she played the piano, then make small talk with her and the residents until it was time to leave.

By Friday though, I was determined to make my move. There was no way I'd survive a whole weekend without seeing her. That afternoon, while Rose played songs like "Somewhere over the Rainbow" and "Moon River," I sat at a table with Letty, filling in some adult coloring books. And by adult, I mean *adult*. Add that to the list of things I had no idea existed. Letty's granddaughter had dropped them off earlier, before I'd arrived.

Letty broke the silence.

"So, you grow some balls yet, kid?"

The tip of my colored pencil snapped off. "What?" I asked.

She let out a soft, throaty chuckle. "You and I both know why you're here every day, and it's not to color, is it?" She nodded toward the piano, then a second time, to emphasize her point.

"What do you mean?" I asked. I knew exactly what she meant.

"Oh, come on, you look over there every ten seconds! And when you're not looking at her, she's looking at you."

I twisted my colored pencil in the sharpener, caught dead to rights. I leaned closer to Letty. "Is it that obvious?"

Letty leaned closer to me. "Does the pope shit in the woods?"

I laughed. "I think it's 'Does a *bear* shit in the woods?' or 'Is the pope *Catholic*?'"

"What'd I say?"

"Neither of those things."

Letty considered this for a moment, then cackled and slapped her knee. "I never was too good at telling other people's jokes."

I was about to respond when Rose appeared out of nowhere. "Hey, how's it going, you two?" she asked.

"Oh, hey! Going well, just . . ."

Just what? Just coloring shirtless *men?*

"Just finishing up," I mumbled.

Letty interrupted. "Sweet Baby Jesus, would you tell her already?"

Rose looked at Letty, then back at me, confused.

I opened my mouth to speak, but nothing came out.

Letty took the stage. "In my day, if a guy wanted a gal, he told her. On the other hand, when I first laid eyes on my Dickey, God rest his soul, I knew what *I* wanted and *I* told *him*." She stood and patted us both on the shoulder. "I'll leave you two alone now." Then she danced away from the table—albeit stiffly—while singing: "*I got rhythm, I got music, I got my man, who could ask for anything more?*"

We watched her shuffle away. Then Rose looked at me shyly.

The saliva suddenly disappeared from my mouth. I blinked and tried to smile, which probably looked more like a snarl. I had two options now: (1) collapse to the ground and explain how my spine had suddenly disappeared or (2) stop snarling and ask Rose to dinner.

Say something nice, ask her out.

"Do you eat dinner?" I blurted at Rose, more aggressively than intended.

Rose jumped. "Dinner?"

I pinched the bridge of my nose and shut my eyes. "I mean you and me."

"You and me?"

Step to the ledge. Don't look down. Take a breath. And . . . jump. "I was thinking we could have dinner together. You and me. At the café. I'll cook." I opened one eye to see how far Rose had run away, but she still stood in front of me.

"Sounds great," she said, hiding a smile.

Relief filled me like a helium balloon. "Great!"

"Tonight?" Rose asked.

"Tonight what?"

"Dinner?"

"Oh, right. Yes. Tonight."

"What time?"

I tried to remember what time people ate dinner. "Six o'clock."

"Perfect! See you soon!"

And with that, Rose walked off to help Candy with craft time.

I reached for my phone to check the time.

No phone.

Dammit.

I checked the clock on the wall.

Five after four.

"Grub!" I yelled, scanning the room. He was off somewhere with Blackjack, no doubt. "*Private* Grub!"

Ever so faintly, the echo of footsteps could be heard running down a hallway. Without missing a beat, I ran toward the sound. I timed it perfectly: Grub reached the end of the hallway the same time I rounded the corner. I swooped him up in my arms, tossed him over my shoulder like a sack of potatoes, and ran for the exit. He may have said something, but I wasn't listening. No time to explain.

As I threw my leg over the Schwinn, I felt his fingers dig into my shoulders. I pedaled as if fleeing an erupting volcano.

I burst through the door of World Peas Café. "Mom . . . café . . . tonight . . . Rose."

Mom placed her hands on her hips and cocked her head to the side, making it look spring-loaded. "Son. Need. Use. Manners."

"Please . . . dinner . . . can't cook . . . need café."

"Mom not robot. Son not ask right."

I took a few deep breaths to regain my ability to speak.

"Rose is coming here. Tonight. At six. I told her I'd cook dinner."

"That's much better." She furrowed her brow while nodding and looking at the floor, finally grasping the gravity of the situation. "So, what is your plan?"

Criminy. Did there have to be a plan for everything?

"I'm working on it," I lied.

Grub stood off to the side, looking slightly worried and windblown.

Mom nodded again, staring off into the middle distance. I could practically see the gears turning behind her eyes as she pondered my predicament. She pursed her lips and nodded, having reached a verdict. "Manny, come with me, we're going to the store. Zeus, go home, take a shower, and change your clothes. Be back here at five thirty and I'll have something started for you."

I looked at my mom—her messy ponytail, her plastic flip-flops, her green-smoothie-splattered clothes. "You know you're the best, right?"

She patted my face and smiled. "I know. Now go get handsome."

FOURTEEN

ROSE KNOCKED ON THE CAFÉ DOOR AT EXACTLY SIX O'CLOCK. MOM HAD closed the shades to keep the setting sun from blinding us through the western-facing windows, or maybe it was to give us some privacy. Either way, I was glad the glass was covered. The café seemed almost romantic in the dim light.

I faced the door and took one final moment to compose myself. I brushed a lock of still-damp hair off my brow and inhaled slow and deep. This was the real deal, a *date* date.

Quick smell check: pass.

Quick breath check: passable.

Quick skills check: adequate.

Good enough.

I swung the door open. It broke free from its slightly off-kilter frame with an obnoxious metallic grunt. Not exactly the cinematic moment I'd hoped for. Rose stood before me, looking radiant, backlit by the early evening sun.

"Good evening," I said, suddenly wishing I hadn't, for the only appropriate follow-up to that is "I vant to suck your blood!"

"Hey there." She grinned at me, making me forget about my less-than-stellar greeting. "You look nice," she said, clearly noticing I wasn't in a faded, sweaty T-shirt for once. Instead, I sported my one and only button-down shirt, a gift from Aunt Willow that had spent most of its existence in the back of my closet. A light green plaid pattern, it featured white pearl snap buttons, short sleeves, and probably could have used a good ironing. But too late for that now.

Say something nice, return the compliment! my brain instructed me.

I looked at Rose, trying to make sure my gaze came across as observant rather than creepy. It was a fine line, one generally defined by the length of time your eyes remain fixed on certain body parts.

She wore a light blue summery dress drawn tight across the middle, accentuating her hips and waist.

Nope, can't comment on that, I thought. *Definitely creepy.*

Her wavy black hair fell upon bare shoulders, her lips a shimmery, soft pink, like the best part of a peach.

Still creepy.

A thin, gold necklace rested above a modest view of cleavage, which, while my favorite feature, I made sure to avoid noticing altogether.

Tap out now, while you're ahead.

"I like that color," I said, nodding in approval at her dress, as if I knew a single thing about fashion or shades of blue. It was a low-risk, low-reward comment, much like saying, "Why, yes, I do enjoy a good nap," or "Cheeseburgers are swell, they are!"

"It's periwinkle."

"It matches your toenails," I noted, looking down at her feet. Several crisscrossing straps held together a pair of thin-soled sandals, from which blue-topped toes poked out.

"How observant," Rose replied. "I brought more nail polish, in case you want to paint your own. You know, to bring out the blue of your eyes."

I flushed then, flattered she'd noticed the color of my eyes. She was obviously much better at this compliment game than I was.

"Great idea. Come on in." I motioned with my arm and she walked past me into the café, the pleasant smell of lotion-perfume-girl-whatever-it-was trailing behind her. I shut the door and flipped on a light, suddenly worried the dimly lit room might qualify for the creepy category.

"You shaved," she observed.

"I did," I said, cupping my face as if just realizing it myself.

"I like it. Let me feel," Rose said, reaching a hand up. She lightly brushed a few fingers along my cheek. "So *smooth*!"

"Thanks," I said, wondering if that was a compliment or a jab.

I led Rose back to the kitchen, where my maiden culinary voyage was about to begin. Once inside, Rose stopped in her tracks. She whipped her head at me. "You did all this?" she asked.

I had to admit—it did look impressive. A package of angel hair pasta sat open next to a full pot of water. A large cutting board displayed a loaf of crusty Italian bread, a wedge of Parmesan, and a crock of herbed butter. Fresh basil lay heaped in a pile next to a bottle of olive oil, a head of garlic, and a bowl of pine nuts. In the corner of the kitchen, a small round table had been covered in a red, checkered cloth, with a single candle in the center, waiting to be lit.

For a split second I considered claiming the work as my own. I opened my mouth, but no words came out.

"Let me guess," said Rose. "You're bound to secrecy under the National Brownie Security Act."

"You're very good at guessing."

"And your mom was very sweet to do this."

"She was," I agreed. "She even left sticky notes all over the place with instructions."

"So where are they?"

"I threw them away. I didn't want you to see them."

Rose let out a laugh, sat at the table, crossed one leg over the other, and folded her hands upon her knee. "Okay then," she said with a big smile. "This is going to be interesting.

What are we having?"

"Pasta with a-pesto and a-garlic bread," I said in an accent that I meant to sound Italian but more closely resembled a cartoon character.

"Mmm, sounds amazing! Is that your specialty?"

"We'll soon find out."

"You've never cooked it before?"

I hesitated before answering. "Not *specifically*."

"So, *unspecifically*?"

Another pause. "Yes."

"Well, I have to say I'm intrigued and confused."

"I have to remain *a little* mysterious."

"Okay, Mr. Mysterious. Let's see what you got."

And for the next hour, I bumbled my way through a series of mistakes. If not for Rose's intervention, we'd have been crunching on raw pasta dipped in ketchup by midnight. Early on, she realized I had absolutely no idea what I was doing and joined in, helping with the process. She demonstrated how a head of garlic was different from a clove, for instance, and the importance of putting a lid on the blender before turning it on.

Despite our combined efforts, the pesto sauce and garlic bread were slight disasters, the former being incredibly pine nut heavy, the latter, blackened bricks. I don't think either of us cared though; we laughed throughout the entire operation, bonding over our attempts to produce something edible.

By the time we sat to eat, the candle had become a stub, more wick than wax.

"That was the best meal I've had all night," said Rose.

"I'm sorry. Next time I'll keep the sticky notes."

"No worries. I enjoy picking pine nuts out of my teeth. And I like my garlic bread properly blackened. God knows what diseases we'd catch from undercooked bread."

The girl was awesome.

"In fact, I'm not sure how you'll ever top this evening, Mr. Gunderson," she continued, leaning back in her chair and crossing her arms.

"Oh, I'm just getting started, Miss Santos," I said, leaning back and crossing my own arms.

"Good, because I happen to be free on Sunday."

"This Sunday?"

"This Sunday."

"As in, the day after tomorrow?"

"The very one."

Hold up, hold up. Did Rose just say she wants to see me two days from now? I mean, the hike was a fluke, tonight was pure luck, but a third date? That means we're, like, a thing, right? As in dating. As in, she may be my girlfriend soon, if I play my cards right?

I remembered what Dylan had told me about confidence. About how girls like it. So I cleared my throat. "This Sunday it is, Miss Santos. Be prepared for an amazing surprise," I said, opening both hands in front of me, like a magician showing the crowd he's not holding any cards.

Which was true. I had no cards to play.

But I did have two days to find some.

FIFTEEN

"WHO STOLE THE KISHKA?" SANG THE ACCORDIONIST. *"WHO STOLE THE kishka? Someone call the cops!"*

A large balding man wearing tall black boots, blue pants, a fluffy white shirt, and a thick sheen of sweat dominated the dance floor with his wife. By dance floor, I mean cracked asphalt shaded by a rent-a-tent, whose perimeter had been decorated with beer-branded pennant flags and a large banner that read *Taube County Polka Festival*.

"Look at them go," said Rose, licking the mustard off her fingers after taking a bite of the sausage we'd split.

"I have to say, I'm impressed," I replied. "This must be the highlight of their year."

Rose looked at me incredulously. "Their *year*? This is the

highlight of my *life*!" We both laughed.

We'd only been at the polka festival for thirty minutes, but it sounded like they'd been playing the same song the entire time. A simple drum kit, a clarinet, a tuba, two trombones, and an accordion were manned by six men in lederhosen, who gently bounced to the rhythm upon a flatbed trailer. The makeshift stage leaned precariously toward the back right corner, making me question the drummer's safety.

"I gotta hand it to you, Zeus," said Rose, tossing a disk-shaped pickle in her mouth. "I didn't see this coming."

"I said you should wear polka dots, but you didn't listen."

"I'll never doubt you again." She handed the boat-shaped cardboard container back to me. "I can now scratch polka festival off my bucket list."

I tossed a pickle in my own mouth and grinned, happy that Rose was happy. Honestly, I'd been a bit worried about my idea at first, but Dylan had been right. You had to be creative around here to find things to do, especially on a budget. So I'd spent the better part of the weekend scrambling to come up with something.

Friday night, after our dinner at the café, Rose and I had walked to the park in the center of town. We sat together on a bench, watching the fountain spurt and bubble around a statue of Abraham Lincoln. We threw in a few pennies and made silent wishes to ourselves. It sounds simple, and it was, but it felt really great. Neither of us wanted the night to end. Instead it went too quickly, as the best ones always do.

Saturday morning, I woke feeling all warm inside. For a moment anyway, until I jumped straight up in bed, realizing the task I'd created for myself. I drank half a pot of coffee—more than twice my normal dosage—which ultimately was more of a hindrance than a help.

After ricocheting around our apartment like a meth-addicted squirrel for hours, I ended up at the café, head in hands, rubbing my temples from the caffeine crash. Mom was too busy to offer any advice, which was okay, since she'd basically orchestrated the entire dinner herself the night before. (Hearing about the evening's success had pleased her to no end.) As I leaned on the counter, something caught my eye. A newspaper lay open to a full-page ad.

Taube County Fiftieth Annual Polka Festival Extravaganza! Food, Music, Beer, Fun! Sunday, June 18, 2:00 p.m.–8:00 p.m. Bring your dancing shoes! Live music by Kyle and the Kielbasas. Free admission!

Bingo!

I tore off the page, and twenty-four hours later, there we sat, sharing a Polish sausage.

"I told you," I said, finishing the last bite. "I'm full of surprises." I wagged my eyebrows at her.

She pointed to her mouth.

I stopped chewing and gaped back at her. *What the hell did that mean? Kiss me? Feed me?*

She tapped her mouth again.

I stared at her blankly and shrugged my shoulders.

"You have mustard on your lip." She dabbed at my mouth with a standard-issue, disintegrate-upon-contact festival napkin as I wavered between embarrassment and pleasure.

The band had moved on to a new verse, *"You can take my shinka, take my long kielbasa,"* to which the crowd sang along.

Without warning, Rose grabbed my hand and led me toward the packed dance floor.

The thought occurred to me—why, for the very first time we held hands, did my fingers have to be stained mustard yellow and slick with grease?

Neither of us were skilled in the art of polka dancing, but aside from the bald man and his wife, no one else seemed to be either. We basically hopped from one foot to the other in unison, my left hand holding her right and my right hand on her upper back. I could feel the heat from her hand where it rested on my shoulder, occasionally squeezing for extra purchase.

Before long, the crowd formed a circle around us, clapping on the downbeat. Even the bald man and his wife stopped to watch, looking quite amused. I knew I had a stupid grin on my face, but I couldn't wipe it off. Rose's eyes had crinkled up, and she wore a grin to match.

I couldn't believe I was (A) at a polka festival; (B) dancing at a polka festival; and (C) not mortified by A or B. I'd hardly danced in my life. But being with Rose made me feel invincible and willing to try things I'd never do otherwise.

As the band revved up for the end, I led Rose into a spin, pulling her into me, her arms crossed in front of her. We fell back in a dip as the music ended, which she accented with a high kick.

The crowd burst into applause. Rose and I took small bows, turning to acknowledge our audience.

Then we looked at each other and burst out laughing. I took her by the hand and led her out of the tent while the band geared up for the next song. We made our way to the edge of the festival grounds, eventually discovering a grove of oak trees shading a narrow creek.

"Over there!" I said, spotting a bench by the trickling water. We sat for a moment, catching our breath.

I pushed the sweaty hair off my forehead. "I don't know about you, but I'm pretty sure we could sweep the school talent show with those moves next year." I looked over to Rose, about to start laughing with her again, but she now wore a troubled look on her face.

Damn. I shouldn't have said that. I'd moved too fast, made assumptions. She was a senior. She wasn't going to date a junior next year. She wasn't going to date *me* next year.

"What is it?" I asked, trying to keep my cool.

She forced a smile. "It's nothing."

"You can tell me," I said, trying to maintain an air of confidence, though inside my anxiety had skyrocketed.

She looked at the water and fiddled with her necklace while I prepped myself for the upcoming rejection.

"So there's this school in New York," she finally said. "It's called the Manhattan Music Conservatory. It's for gifted young musicians."

"Like you," I said, nodding as if I understood where this was headed.

Rose shrugged. "Like a lot of people. So anyway, I got accepted this past spring and wait-listed for a scholarship, but it's not a sure thing. It's really expensive and there's no way I can go without financial aid."

"That's rough," I said sympathetically, though inside I felt myself relax. Not that I wanted to think about her going away to college in a year, but at least she wasn't giving me the "let's just be friends" talk. "You still have a whole year to work out the kinks; I'm sure you'll be able to figure something out," I continued.

She bit her lip. "Zeus, the conservatory isn't a college, it's a high school. If I get the scholarship, I'll leave in August. *This* August. Two months from now."

I felt my insides go numb. I knew it. This had all been too good to be true. She was leaving me already. I wanted to beg her not to go, but how long had we known each other? Two weeks?

Two weeks ago *I* would have jumped at the chance to leave Buffalo Falls. How could I blame her?

I tried to hide my devastation with fake enthusiasm. "Wow, your senior year in New York City. That sounds amazing!"

"It's what I've been hoping for, dreaming about for months now." She gave a small smile then, and the little dimple under her lip appeared, breaking my heart in two.

Don't go, don't go, don't go.

"That's awesome, Rose! I hope the scholarship comes through."

I wasn't even sure what I was saying, but it felt like all the right things. I saw relief wash over her face. Her smile widened.

God, that smile. I never wanted it to go away. But I guess I'd take it for as long as I could have it.

I smiled back.

"Thank you, Zeus. I've actually been really worried about telling you."

"I'm pretty scary," I said, raising an eyebrow.

She laughed and gave me a playful shove. "Why are you so sweet to me?"

While I wanted to put my arm around her, I shoved her back instead. "Because I like you, Rose."

Immediately, the blood rushed to my face. I felt like I had returned to fifth grade and checked off the Yes box on a "Do you like me?" note. The water trickled, the leaves rustled, a crow cawed, and my heart beat in my ears for an eternity while I awaited a response.

"I like you, too," Rose said, "but—"

Oh God. Now what. "But—?"

"But now you've totally outdone yourself, Mr. Gunderson. How will you ever top the Taube County Fiftieth Annual Polka Festival Extravaganza?"

Sorry, God. False alarm.

"That was just a warm-up, Miss Santos," I said, my fear replaced with reckless optimism. "How about this—every Sunday for the rest of the summer I'll surprise you with something new. Even if you do leave in August, I'll show you the best summer you've ever had in Buffalo Falls."

"That sounds like a challenge."

No kidding. Something new every Sunday for the rest of the summer? Was that even possible? The most likely ending was that I'd run out of ideas, Rose would fly off to New York, and I'd be left behind with random mustard stains and a truckload of pain.

Still.

Two months with Rose.

I stuck my hand across the bench.

She met it with hers.

"Deal?" I asked.

"Deal."

SIXTEEN

"THE MISSING PIECES HAVE TO BE HERE SOMEWHERE. DID YOU CHECK the floor?" Letty asked the following Thursday. She shuffled around the table where the puzzle we'd spent the last half hour on was laid out.

"Yes, still not on the floor."

"For cryin' out loud, we need to find Eduardo's frank and beans."

I knew where they were, of course. But I felt no one would be happy if Missy Stouffer were to walk over and find a nude, muscle-bound man named Eduardo sitting atop his motorcycle. That's why I'd been smuggling select puzzle pieces to my lap, so that only the motorcycle, the asphalt, the sky, and some less-offensive parts of Eduardo were visible on the table.

"I don't know, Letty, looks like we're missing some pieces. We should probably call the company for a refund," I said, trying to find a way out of finishing the puzzle.

"Well, damn." Letty once again looked at the box lid, which displayed the complete Eduardo, minus his man parts, which were covered with a disturbingly large black censor box.

As I slipped another piece in my lap, a Nerf dart hit me in the side of the head, followed by *"BZSHOO!"*

I turned to see Grub in position behind a chair, reloading.

"Fire!" yelled Blackjack as Mary Santos rolled him into view. *"BZSHOO!"*

"Hey, watch the friendly fire." I stood to pick up the two Nerf darts as bits of Eduardo spilled from my lap to the floor.

"Aha!" said Letty, pointing as they fell.

I shrugged my shoulders. "Hi, Mary." I gave Blackjack a quick salute, which he returned. Grub was still partially hidden behind a chair.

"Hi, Zeus," said Mary. "These two have had quite the time today," she said, motioning to Grub and Blackjack. "Blackjack got to telling some stories even *I've* never heard. They've become real comrades lately." Then she leaned in so only I could hear. "Blackjack's having one of his *good* days."

I gave a quick nod of understanding. Over the past week, Mary and I had each talked to Grub regarding Blackjack and the nature of his illness. We'd explained how Alzheimer's not only affected Blackjack's memory, but how it could also confuse him or alter his mood. And though Mary often marveled at Blackjack's improvement since befriending Grub, she still cautioned that on *bad* days, Blackjack needed to be alone.

I smiled at the old man. "How are you today, Sergeant?"

"Me? Never felt better. Let me tell you, this brother of yours is smart as a whip," he said in his slow, deep voice. "I think he knows more about the war than I do. Isn't that right, soldier?"

Grub stepped out from behind the chair, and Blackjack beamed at him with pride.

"He talks about you all the time," I said. "He loves hearing your World War II stories."

"Well, I sure enjoy his company."

"Sergeant Porter and I went on a mission," said Grub, chiming in.

"A mission, huh?" I said.

Mary gave me a grin. "I let your brother push Blackjack around the staff lounge while I finished my reports."

"Sounds like a very important mission," I said.

"He's teaching me how to sneak up on the enemy," replied Grub.

"Yes, and they like to pretend *I'm* the enemy," said Mary, laughing. "Isn't that right, Blackjack?"

"You want to be our ally, Mary, then stop foisting that tapioca pudding on us. We like *butterscotch*, woman. How many times we gotta tell you?"

Blackjack shot Grub a wink then. Grub giggled.

Mary smiled and patted the top of Grub's army helmet. "You two are incorrigible. But now it's time for Sergeant Porter's nap."

The comrades exchanged salutes, and Mary wheeled Blackjack away. "Glad you and Rose had fun at the polka festival last Sunday, Zeus," she called back to me.

"Polka festival?" Letty asked, rising from under the table where she'd been retrieving Eduardo's man parts. "Taube County?"

I waved to Mary, then turned to Letty. "Yep. Rose and I went on Sunday."

Letty dropped the pile of pieces in the empty center of the puzzle and began assembling them, to my horror. "You probably saw half my damn family there."

"Oh yeah? I was telling my friend Dylan about you the other day and he said he hangs out with two of your great-grandkids."

"Kid, you can't fart in this town without a Kowalczyk walking through the cloud. Which ones?"

"Axl and uh—"

"Novie."

"Right, Novie. They play in a band together."

Letty harrumphed. "Sure, they have a band, and my ass isn't saggy. They make plenty of noise, I'll give you that."

I tried not to picture her ass. "They're twins, right? I hear Axl plays bass and Novie plays—"

"Loud. That girl's been beating on pots and pans since she fell out of her mother."

"Drums, that's right," I said, not sure of the appropriate response.

"Their mother, Christy—that's my granddaughter, of course—everyone calls her Crash."

"Why's that?"

Letty laughed to herself. "She had some wild years. I'll let you fill in the blanks. Anyway, she owns the Beauty Saloon downtown. Half bar, half beauty salon. Very clever name, I'll give her that. Can't say the same for those poor kids of hers."

"I'm actually getting together with them to jam at Dylan's house tomorrow night."

"Jam? You mean make a racket?"

"Something like that. I've been learning guitar."

"Have you?" Letty eagerly grabbed my hand. "Do you know any Tom Jones?"

"Sorry, not yet."

"Damn. Well, as soon as you do, you get in here and play it for me." She released my hand and gave it a soft pat, then turned back to the puzzle. "Here we are. Eduardo's almost a man now."

"No!" I shouted as Grub approached the table, a now fully formed (minus one important piece) Eduardo smiling back.

"Here's a map of the battlefield," said Grub. He opened a piece of paper the size of a newspaper across the table, covering Eduardo.

I gave Letty a playful stink eye. "That was close."

Letty shrugged. "It's like I always say, kiddo—enjoy today, you might be dead tomorrow!"

It was true. She *did* always say it. And I'd decided it wasn't necessarily bad advice. Ever since Rose had told me she might be moving to New York City in August, the countdown in my head had begun. I kept telling myself to not think about it, to focus on the time I had with her here and not worry about her living there.

It didn't always work though. I moped a lot when I wasn't with her. But what good did that do?

Letty was right.

Enjoy today, you might be dead tomorrow.

Maybe I'd make that my new mantra.

Grub spent the next several minutes showing us locations on the map of enemy bunkers, watchtowers, and traps.

"Well done, kid, well done," Letty said when he was finished. "You run a tight ship. They ought to put you in charge of this place instead of that stick in the mud, Ms. Muffinstuffer."

Grub, pleased by the compliment, went back to his map. I said a quick prayer of thanksgiving that Ms. Stouffer was across the room and Rose was playing a particularly upbeat show tune.

"So how are things going with your cutie-patootie over there?" Letty asked, tilting her head toward the piano.

"Great," I replied. "Thought I might take her to a movie this week, but I'm not exactly loaded and I hear the old theater seats downtown are ground zero for head lice and ringworm."

"*And* back injuries. Not to mention that floor is stickier than a motel mattress. You know what you should do?" Letty said, snapping her fingers at me. "You two should come to movie night here instead. Every other Thursday, which is tonight. They're always needing volunteers. It's free, and we get ice cream cups!"

She almost had me at "free," but I wasn't so sure. Rose had been a great sport about the polka festival, but movie night at a nursing home? That had to rate a zero on the romantic scale.

Letty must have noticed my concern.

"Trust me, kiddo, half this place will be snoozing before the credits roll. It'll be like no one's here."

"Sold."

SEVENTEEN

THURSDAY EVENING ROSE AND I ARRIVED AT HILLTOP TWENTY MIN-utes before show time. Mom had loaned me the Lego so I could pick up Rose. During the short drive to Hilltop, Rose teased me about taking her on a date to the nursing home—clearly not the smoothest move—but I could tell by her smile that she felt the same way I did.

As long as we were together, it didn't matter what we did. Or *where.*

The common room looked better than I'd expected. The furniture had been rearranged to face the wall, upon which the title screen of Pixar's *Up* was projected. The drapes had been drawn over the tall windows to block out the evening sun. The recessed ceiling lights glowed bright. After the past few weeks, the big room, with its high ceiling and oversized couches, now felt familiar to me, like an old pair of jeans.

Rose and I stood at the back of the gathering, looking for two open seats.

"There, next to the Larsens on the red couch." Rose pointed to a spot in the back of the crowd, where one of Hilltop's few married couples sat together. The majority of the residents had been widowed, but a few who were lucky and able enough shared rooms with their spouses.

George and Lucille Larsen greeted us with big smiles, as if nothing could have pleased them more than to share a couch with us. Lucille sported a white George Washington–meets–Dutch Boy hairdo and glasses so thick they magnified her eyes to the size of the lenses. Her counterpart, George, not a day under eighty-five, had a full head of bushy gray hair, argyle socks hiked up to his knees, and khaki shorts belted high across his belly, further supported by suspenders as a secondary safety measure.

"Make yourselves comfortable!" yelled Lucille at a volume indicating substantial hearing loss. "You see that, George? We have a new guest."

George, who hadn't heard a word, replied, "Where's the ice cream?"

"*New. Guests.*" Lucille pointed to us, speaking slow and loud, right into George's ear.

George pointed at his mouth. "*Ice. Cream.*"

Whether or not they ever did hear each other remained

unclear, which was perhaps the secret to their sixty years of marriage.

Just then Candy wheeled in the cart of ice cream cups.

Rose and I hopped up to help—a small price to pay for free entertainment.

"You don't know how much I appreciate you two volunteering for this," Candy said, flashing us a grateful smile. "We're making friendship bracelets tomorrow for craft time and I've got a thousand beads to sort out before then. I'll be cross-eyed by the time I'm done."

"Happy to help," I said, taking the cart from her.

"Super! I brought you extra napkins. The ice cream can get messy at times," Candy said, handing me a large sheaf of napkins and a roll of paper towels. "Holler if you need anything!" she added with a wave, then double-timed it down the hallway in her neon-pink Crocs.

I looked at Rose. "Is it just me, or did Candy seem especially eager to get the hell out of here?" I asked.

Rose grinned and took the napkins from me. "Maybe she's just really excited to sort beads."

"Right."

And so, one tray at a time, Rose and I distributed ice cream cups to the Hilltop residents. The ice cream was the same as I remembered from grade school—ribbed, plastic cups filled with vanilla ice cream and a swirl of strawberry or chocolate that looked like a five-pointed star. Each came with a small wooden paddle for scooping.

Once we got everyone situated with their ice cream, paddles, napkins, and a few makeshift paper towel bibs, I dimmed the lights and Rose pushed play. A short Pixar film about storks delivering babies began to roll.

Rose and I had just settled back into our seats when she nudged me and motioned to her right. A woman in white poodle curls and wire-frame glasses had been parked next to us in a wheelchair. A lace collar poked out of her oversized beige cardigan, the sleeves rolled up to reveal two whisper-thin hands that shook so badly she could barely feed herself.

"Come on, let's help," Rose whispered.

We ducked, so as not to block anyone's view, and scooted over to the woman, crouching on either side of her.

"Here, Vera, we'll give you a hand," said Rose.

I guess I'd expected Rose to help, while I supplied the moral support, but when Rose picked up the ice cream and handed me the wooden paddle, my role became clear. I didn't mind.

"You're very kind," said Vera. "I never used to shake like this, but now, well, you see . . ."

"It's okay," I whispered. "We don't mind."

And to my surprise, I really didn't. Sure, I'd first volunteered at Hilltop purely to be around Rose. But that night, right then, I had a realization, one that had been sneaking up on me for days, subtle and slow, the way dusk turns to night.

I truly cared about the Hilltop residents.

They weren't kooky old people, as I'd originally seen them, but *real* people. Real people who were once young and independent. Real people who had dreams and fears, who had lived and loved and suffered.

Still suffered, some of them. Like Vera.

They couldn't help the circumstances of their age any more than I could help mine.

And so I fed Vera her strawberry ice cream while Rose dabbed at her mouth with a napkin. It felt awkward at first, but as it went on, all three of us were giggling like little kids. When we were finished, I grabbed the blanket hanging from the back of Vera's wheelchair and tucked it over her legs.

"Thank you, dear," she said, placing a warm hand on my arm.

I made a mental note to spend more time with her in the future.

Rose and I settled back into our spot on the couch next to Lucille and George, who had already fallen asleep, just as Letty had predicted. George's ice cream cup lay empty upon his belly, slowly rising up and down with each breath. I smiled to myself.

The movie, *Up*, which Rose had already seen, had reached a montage scene of a couple falling in love, getting married, and growing old together. Rose leaned over and warned me, "It's going to get sad," to which I, as a red-blooded American male said, "No problem." I never cried at movies.

Five minutes later, tears were rolling down my face.

"I told you," said Rose, dabbing at her eyes.

I discreetly tried to wipe my face with a napkin. "It's from all the Lysol," I explained, wondering who the hell had picked this movie for a bunch of old people anyway.

"Sure it is," she teased. Then she leaned over and rested her head upon my shoulder. My right arm was propped on the couch armrest, and the wooden frame was jabbing into my ribs. In fact, I'd been about to shift positions just before this new circumstance arose. But now, I had the endurance of a hundred men, the strength of a bull, and the body of Eduardo, the X-rated puzzle man.

I held out my left hand, palm up, and prayed, never taking my eyes off the screen. A moment later, skin met skin, and her hand was in mine. I closed my fingers, and she did the same. My heart pounded.

I gave her hand a squeeze.

She squeezed back.

EIGHTEEN

BEFORE LEAVING HOME FRIDAY NIGHT, I RECEIVED A FULL-SCALE psychological evaluation, interrogation, and downright cross-examination from my mom. She folded laundry while I leaned on the doorframe, answering questions that came in rapid-fire succession.

"Who's going to be there?" she asked.

"Dylan, and his two friends, Axl and Novie," I answered.

"Will an adult be there?"

"Yeah, Dylan's sister, Maggie. She's, like, twenty-four."

"No parents?"

"Dylan's parents are spending the summer in India."

"And left him alone?"

"Like I said, his sister will be there."

"Will there be alcohol?"

"I don't know."

"You don't know?"

"I'm not bringing any."

"Well, that's reassuring," Mom replied, sounding slightly irritated. "How do I know the other kids won't be drinking?"

"I guess you don't know. I'm not going there to drink. I'm going there to hang out and play music."

"Will Rose be there?"

"No. I asked her, but she has to practice for her piano lesson tomorrow."

"I see."

"You see?"

My mom turned to face me with an "I know something you haven't learned yet" look that made me feel about six years old. "Yes, *I see*. And you'll be needing the car, I suppose?"

"I can't ride my bike across town carrying a guitar. Plus, it'll be dark on the way home."

"Oh, it will? And how long do you plan on staying?"

"I don't know, until we're done jamming."

"Try ten o'clock."

"*Ten?!* How about midnight?"

"Ten."

"Eleven."

"Ten."

"Ten thirty."

"Ten."

Apparently going on dates with Rose = safe and harmless; jamming with friends = dangerous and deadly. Finally, I conceded and threw my guitar in the back seat and drove across town to Dylan's. Halfway there I began to feel nervous, as if the whole idea was a huge mistake. I wished Rose was going to be there; she always found a way to put me at ease. I'd be seeing her Sunday though. I still needed to come up with a surprise, but I had all day Saturday for that.

I pulled up to Dylan's house and parked on the street. A rusted Ford pickup truck that had once been red but had faded to a dull, orangish hue sat in the driveway. In the bed of the truck, a large black speaker cabinet lay on its side. Various shiny metal stands, which I assumed belonged to a drum kit, sat in a pile next to the speaker. Suddenly, I felt ill equipped for my first official jam session, having only my acoustic guitar with no amplifier or accessories whatsoever.

Too late to back out now, I thought.

I walked to the front door and knocked. Dylan's sister, Maggie, greeted me and let me inside.

"How was BuffaloFest?" she asked while walking me through the kitchen to the basement stairs. I heard the muffled sounds of voices from below.

"It was cool. I met a ton of people."

"I bet you did. D knows everybody." Maggie stopped and pointed at me. "He didn't go on his goldfish rant, did he?"

I laughed. "Yeah, maybe a little bit."

"Oh, *God*, I don't think he'll ever let that go." Maggie laughed and shook her head. "They're all down there. Not too loud, okay?"

"No problem. Thanks again for the wristbands."

"Sure thing."

Half the basement had been sectioned off by two old couches and a couple of recliners. In the center, a wooden trunk had become a makeshift table, covered with stacks of magazines, printed lyrics, and a few open bags of chips. A drum kit sat half-assembled in the corner. Vampire Weekend played from a speaker where someone's phone had been docked to the port on top.

"Zeus, what's up, man!" said Dylan, waving to me from one of the couches. "Axl, Novie, this is the guitar player I was telling you about."

"Hey guys," I replied. I felt naked standing there with just my acoustic guitar. I wished I at least had a carrying case for it, or an amp.

"What's up, Zeus?" asked Novie. She lay on the other couch, a *Drummer's Digest* magazine spread across her stomach. White-blond hair fanned her face, the tips looking like they'd been dipped in a purple inkwell.

"Hey, man," said Axl, who sat cross-legged on the floor beneath her. He shared the same fair hair and wide cheekbones as his twin, and both had inherited Letty's crystal-blue eyes.

"Have a seat," Dylan said, making room for me on the couch.

Agatha lay on the floor in front of him, looking exhausted from her day of being a dog.

"So, Zeus," Axl began, "where do you get a name like that? Your parents into Greek mythology or something?"

"Let me guess," said Novie. "You have a sister named Aphrodite and a brother named Poseidon."

"I wish." I laughed. "My brother's name is Manuel Thor Gunderson, no joke. I call him Grub. Mine's even worse—Jesús Bjorn Gunderson, so I go by Zeus."

"Right on, makes sense," Axl said.

"Yeah, my mom basically cursed us in the name department," I replied. "Speaking of that, what's up with Axl and Novie?"

The twins gave each other a look, one I realized they had shared many times.

"Perhaps I can explain in song," said Dylan. He flipped on an amp, grabbed a guitar, and began to sing. *"Nothing lasts forever, and we both know hearts can change. And it's hard to hold a candle in the cold November rain."*

"Stop!" Novie covered her face with a pillow as if to smother the song out of her head. Dylan played a little lick on guitar and laughed.

"Wait, really?" I said, starting to put the puzzle together.

"Really," said Axl. "Meet November Rain Gunther, aka Novie."

"And that would make you Axl *Rose* Gunther?" I asked.

"Haha!" Novie pointed and laughed at her brother from under the pillow.

"I thought Jesús Bjorn was bad," I said.

"It's pretty bad," said Axl.

"Definitely stick with Zeus," said Dylan.

"So your parents are huge Guns N' Roses fans, I take it?" I asked.

"Mom is, yeah. She used to be, anyway," said Novie. "She had a thing for eighties bands."

"To our everlasting shame," Axl added.

"Your mom . . . So that's Letty's granddaughter, right? Crash?" I asked.

"That's her, Christy 'Crash' Liszieski," said Novie. "'The crazy skips every other generation, so we didn't get it.'"

"Yep, no crazy here," said Axl.

"Right. No crazy here at all," said Dylan, thick on the sarcasm.

"Dylan doesn't get to be in our Horrible Names Club," said Novie.

"Really? Come on! I was named after a poet, doesn't that count for anything?"

The two other members of the Horrible Names Club and I shook our heads no.

"Dammit," said Dylan.

"I'm also a proud Mexiwegian," I pointed out. "Beat that."

"Mexiwegian?" Novie asked.

"Half Mexican, half Norwegian. Mexiwegian."

Novie turned to her brother. "What would that make us? Mom's Polish, what's Dad?"

"Mostly German, I think," said Axl.

"So you're Germish," I said.

"I knew it! Keep those scabies and tapeworms to yourselves," Dylan said, leaning away from the twins.

For the next hour, conversation flowed freely. My initial discomfort melted away as soon as we started trading funny stories about our weird families—we were more alike than I'd expected. I found out that Axl and Novie's dad had moved to Alaska when they were babies, and they only talked to him once a year at Christmas. Dylan talked about his New Age parents and their large collection of Reiki stones and essential oils. And even though I'd never told anyone else but Rose, I explained how my mom had decided to skip the sperm donor bank and get knocked up for free in Latin America.

Twice.

It felt good to be around people who didn't judge me, who had stories as strange as my own. And it felt good to laugh about it. What else could we do?

Eventually, we got around to playing music. I helped Axl and Novie drag their equipment in from the pickup truck and navigate it through the house, careful not to put any holes in the drywall. Dylan stayed in the basement, setting up microphones on stands. Duct tape was heavily featured in their assembly.

They kindly asked me what songs I knew, to which I replied that I'd play whatever they wanted. They'd all know soon enough how much I sucked.

Dylan ended up showing us a song he'd recently written. It only had three chords: E minor, C, and D—right in my wheelhouse—so I gently strummed along. I tried to keep up, but I played really soft, afraid I'd mess up. It probably turned out to be a good thing I wasn't amplified, but I think I held my own. Axl and Novie listened while tapping their feet and bobbing their heads.

"That's awesome, man," said Dylan, when we came to the end. "We've been needing a rhythm guitarist."

Rhythm guitarist. Had a nice ring to it.

"Thanks," I replied. "I kind of screwed up that middle part."

"No, you didn't! You were great!" said Novie.

"Yeah, dude. Spot on," said Axl.

I didn't know if they were serious, or just being nice.

"Here, try this out." Dylan opened up a black case and pulled out a dark blue Fender Telecaster.

Like Joe Strummer's, I thought. *Almost.*

Dylan plugged it into an amp and handed it to me.

"Um . . ." I said.

"Here's your volume," Dylan said, pointing to a knob, "this

chooses your pickup, and this adjusts your treble and bass."

"Got it," I replied, though I felt out of my league. I strummed a chord and jumped at how loud it was.

Dylan laughed. "Don't worry, she won't bite ya."

I turned the volume knob and strummed again. Much better.

After that, Axl showed us a bass line he'd been working on. I watched in awe as Dylan put his head down and worked his way up and down the neck of his own guitar to find the matching chords. I studied his hands closely. *Okay, I recognize that one, I think that's an F. That's definitely a C. I think that's an A minor. No! D minor. Now A minor. I know that's a G.* I followed along the best I could. After about five or six times through the chord progression, I had it down.

Novie tapped out the tempo on the hi-hat, then fell into a groove with the snare and kick drum.

Dylan watched me play, which made me nervous, but soon he nodded at me in approval. Then he clicked a pedal on the floor and launched into a guitar solo.

Holy shit.

I was actually playing with a band.

I could *feel* the bass, *feel* the kick drum. My own guitar was part of the music, almost like a conversation. There was a sense of collectivity, a unity. This was what I wanted. This was what I *needed*.

We finally reached the big ending, accented by heavy cymbal crashes and me breaking a string.

I didn't care though.

My ears were ringing, my fingers were bleeding, and I couldn't wipe the stupid grin off my face.

NINETEEN

THE PSYCHIC'S HEAD WHIPPED UP, HER EYES OPEN WIDE. "THAT'S THE old-soul line, right there."

"It is?" asked Rose.

"Yes. You've lived many past lives."

"I have?"

"Mm-hmm." Mo the psychic traced a line along Rose's palm from below her index finger to her wrist. "You will live near a large body of water. Soon. Within the next six months."

"Really?" said Rose. "Is it the ocean?"

"Hard to say," replied Mo.

"So it could be any body of water?" I chimed in. "I mean, it could be a river or a lake too, right?"

Mo flashed me a look. "Yes, it could," she finally said, after staring into my soul for a moment.

Mo owned Moira's Psychic Healing and Palm Reading, the business located down the strip mall from World Peas Café. The previous night, I'd brought her some leftovers from the café, which apparently my mom had been dropping off for weeks. It was then I'd come up with the idea to surprise Rose with a palm reading on Sunday. I'd half expected—okay, I'd fully expected—to find an old woman in a silk gown and a shiny jewel-encrusted turban speaking in some gypsy accent as she hovered over a crystal ball. It turned out that to be a psychic in Buffalo Falls, all you needed were a pair of tie-dyed shoes, some tarot cards, and a twenty-by-ten-foot office space. Forest green, soul-sucking animal eyes didn't hurt either.

I decided to keep my mouth shut for the rest of the reading.

Mo continued to stare at Rose's hands, which rested on the table in front of her, palms up.

"You were an artist in a past life. A painter, perhaps. Possibly a musician."

"I play piano now, in this life," Rose replied.

Mo looked Rose in the eyes. "I know."

"Psychic," I mouthed, pointing at Mo.

"Oh, right," said Rose.

Mo stared for a moment, then pointed to a spot on Rose's right palm. "There. These two lines connect here. Is there someone new in your life?"

Rose gave me a look. Her eyebrows twitched and her lips pursed like she was trying to hold in a smile. "Yes," she answered.

Mo glanced at me, then looked back to Rose and referenced me with a head tilt, meaning, "That guy there?"

Rose nodded.

Mo scrunched up her face. I think it was a sign of approval, but it could have been "Oh well" or "He'll do."

Maybe both.

"All right, that's all. Next. You're up." Mo was looking at me.

"That's okay. This was just for her—"

"Have a seat." Mo motioned to where Rose was sitting, with an air of authority that didn't leave much room for debate.

Long story short, when she told me to sit, I sat.

I rested the backs of my hands on the table and stared down at them, waiting for the process to begin. She said nothing. I flexed my fingers, straightening them, offering her a better look at my palms.

Still nothing.

I looked up to find her staring at my face, her brow furrowed into a twisted knot, her crazy eyes burning into the very essence of my being. I think I jumped a little. I looked back down at my hands, then up to her. Her face hadn't changed.

I cleared my throat. "So, what do you see?" I asked, breaking the silence.

Mo leaned back in her chair, crossed her arms over her chest, and threw one leg over the other.

"You need to do some meditating," she finally said.

"I do?"

"White light."

"White light?"

"Surround yourself in white light." She made a lasso motion above her head, indicating such.

My arms trembled now from holding my palms up. I wasn't sure if I should release the position yet. "White light," I repeated.

"You have a spiritual blockage," she said, in the way someone might say, "Your fly's open."

"I had leftover pizza for breakfast, it's probably just that," I said, but Mo didn't laugh.

Rose suppressed a snicker.

"I'm serious. You need to meditate. Surround yourself in white light to keep the bad spirits out."

"Got it. So do you see anything in my future?" I asked. "Besides the spiritual blockage, I mean."

Mo looked to Rose and back to me. Then her face untwisted. She leaned on the table with her elbows. "I see a long walk. I see a sunny afternoon. I see holding hands. I see smiling faces." Her face released into a Grinch-like grin, showcasing her smoke-stained teeth. "But you didn't need me to tell you that, did you?"

Mo didn't charge us for the visit. She said as long as my mom kept sending the leftovers, we could come back for a free reading anytime.

Rose gave me plenty of guff for my psychic shortcomings the second we were out the door. I didn't have much ammo for retaliation since Mo had been spot-on with Rose's reading. The first thing she'd said when Rose sat down was "You bring joy to people's lives." I obviously couldn't argue that point. She'd also been right about the musician thing, and even about living by a large body of water in the near future, though I tried not to think about it. Rose and I had spent the last week avoiding the topic of the Manhattan Music Conservatory, and I was glad to do so.

Enjoy today, you might be dead tomorrow.

Rose and I walked hand in hand through downtown Buffalo Falls. We didn't have anything else to do that day, and Mo's premonition of a long walk seemed like a good idea. Puffy white clouds dotted the sapphire sky, occasionally providing shade as they drifted in front of the sun. A digital sign hung from a bank over the sidewalk, letting us know it was seventy-eight degrees—just right.

We passed a playground overrun with little kids who looked to be around Grub's age. It was a birthday party. I tried to picture my brother playing with them—climbing across the monkey bars, going down the slide, on the swing set—but all I could picture was him belly-crawling around the perimeter with his Nerf gun.

I smiled to myself.

"What?" Rose asked.

"I was just thinking about my brother, and how since moving here his best friend is a ninety-one-year-old Alzheimer's patient. What's with that?"

"It's kind of sweet though."

"It is," I admitted, "but I feel bad for him, too. He actually had friends his own age in Chicago. Now all he talks about are his missions with Blackjack."

"It's probably just his way of coping with the change."

"I guess."

We crossed a street and passed a small bookstore where a short-haired girl our age was cleaning the glass on the other side of the window. She smiled when she saw Rose and waved at us.

We waved back.

"Friend of yours?"

Rose nodded. "Tracie. She was my first friend here. I didn't know a single person and I felt so out of place—we were the only Filipino family in Buffalo Falls. For the first few days of school I didn't know who to sit with at lunch so I went to the library instead. One day, this girl sits down next to me and slides me a book of poetry by Mary Oliver. We've been friends ever since."

"She sounds great."

"She is. Super smart, kind of quiet, but really funny once you get to know her."

"Sounds like someone I know," I said, lightly leaning my shoulder into hers.

Rose leaned back and suppressed a smile. "Is that so?"

"Very so."

We waited for a stoplight, then headed through the downtown park, passing the Lincoln fountain where we'd made wishes the night of our dinner disaster. It seemed like forever ago and yesterday at the same time.

"Don't worry, I'm sure Grub will be fine," said Rose, circling back to our earlier conversation. "He's a good kid. He'll find a friend his own age soon. Someone who appreciates his quirks and charms."

I chuckled. "That's a nice way of putting it. I hope you're right."

"I'm *always* right, Mr. Gunderson."

"Does always being right qualify as a quirk or a charm, Miss Santos?"

"Both."

"I suppose you're right."

"See?"

We walked for over an hour, never once letting go of each other's hands. Occasionally, I'd squeeze her palm and she'd squeeze back, silent code for "I'm here" and "I'm here, too."

As we approached the four-lane bridge leading over the Stone River, Rose asked me if I believed in dreams.

"You mean the ones where your teeth fall out? Or you're suddenly at school in your underwear?"

"Ha, you have those, too?"

"Way too often."

"They're the worst. But I don't mean *those*, specifically. Just dreams in general."

"Sleeping dreams, or 'what you want to do with your life' dreams?"

"I don't know, both."

I thought about it for a bit before answering. "This morning, I dreamed I was lying on a twin bed in a dark room. There wasn't anything else in the room except for me and that bed. But then I noticed a little kid, maybe two years old, sitting on a blanket on the floor across from me. At first, I couldn't figure out who he was, but then I realized—the little kid was me."

"So you were both people in your dream?"

"Yes, and it gets weirder. The kid looks at me and says, 'Hi, Zeus,' and I reply, 'Hi, Zeus.' So, you know, I'm having this conversation with my younger self. And then I start thinking, oh my God, I have to tell my younger self all the things that will happen to him. To *me*. I have to tell him that when he's in third grade he should avoid the sixth grader on the bus who'll punch him, and that he'll have a brother in a few years who will be a little odd, but he'll love him anyway, and that when he's sixteen he's going to move to a new town and he won't want to, but it'll be worth it because he'll meet this awesome girl there."

Rose squeezed my hand again.

"And I'm telling my younger self all of these things, but it's like he's not understanding. *I'm* not understanding. I'm like, 'Listen man, I'm giving you the answers, I *know* what's going to happen to you and you're just sucking your thumb.' And then I woke up."

Rose didn't say anything, but turned her head and looked at me.

"What?" I asked. "What do you think it means?"

"You have a spiritual blockage," Rose said, in the same voice as Mo the psychic. "Surround yourself in white light," she continued, making a lasso motion around her head.

"Okay, okay," I said, nudging her with my shoulder. "I need some spiritual Ex-Lax and a strobe light. So, what about you? Do you believe in dreams?"

Rose shrugged, then let go of my hand and walked to the railing, which was chin high. Traffic zoomed behind us, and below, a barge floated by carrying what looked to be mulch. Rose had her elbows up on the rail, and her chin rested on her hands. I took a mental picture, to remember it later. "I don't know," she replied. "How do you know which dreams are real? How do you know which ones to believe in?"

I paused. "I guess you don't know. You just believe in what feels right."

Rose stared down at the water, then turned and grabbed both of my hands. "This feels right." She smiled at me and tilted her head back the tiniest bit.

For once, I knew exactly what to do.

I leaned in and kissed her.

She slid her hands around my neck, holding me closer. I put one hand on her hip and pushed her hair back over her ear with the other, cupping her face. Our tongues met, sending a rush through my whole body.

After what felt like minutes, but was probably three seconds, a car drove by honking its horn, causing us to separate.

"Well then," said Rose in a whisper, a sparkle in her eyes.

"Well then," I replied.

We spent the rest of the afternoon lounging at the riverfront park, mostly lying on a picnic table, gazing at the sky. Boaters puttered by, seagulls screeched in search of human handouts, and a few fishermen sat at the river's edge. Now that the floodgates had been opened, our make-out sessions came freely and with short intermissions. The sky had turned a deep purple by the time Rose called her mom for a ride.

TWENTY

I WON'T GO INTO GRAPHIC DETAILS, BUT I WILL SAY THIS: WHETHER ON a park bench or in the odd broom closet at Hilltop, Rose and I made the best possible use of our time together, which had increased exponentially since we'd visited the psychic. I'd hardly been home the past week except to sleep, since we'd started spending every evening together, too. I've never gone through so many breath mints and ChapStick tubes in my life.

Meanwhile, Grub and Blackjack had become nearly inseparable at Hilltop, making it easier for me to steal moments with Rose. Blackjack loved "playing army" with Grub, and Grub couldn't have asked for a better partner. Blackjack had been having some really good days lately, and Mary allowed them a bit more freedom together while it lasted.

Admittedly, it was an odd sight—a little boy in army clothes pushing an old guy in a wheelchair, both rattling off battle cries and military jargon. People stopped and saluted them when they rolled by, all except for Missy Stouffer, who eyed them warily. But that seemed to be her typical reaction to everyone and everything.

Speaking of Ms. Stouffer, she'd finally backed off my case a bit since I'd proven my worth as a volunteer bunion rubber and puzzle assembler. Many of the residents knew me by name now, and my romance with Rose was quite the topic of interest. Being at the top of the social pyramid, Letty informed everyone of all new developments. I never gave her too many details out of respect for Rose's privacy, but her incessant prodding during my volunteer time usually meant I told her more than I'd intended.

On Thursday, Rose and I stood outside the exercise room while a visiting instructor attempted to teach beginning yoga poses to those residents brave enough to try. The elderly Hill-toppers mostly giggled, groaned, and tooted, except for Letty, the lithest eighty-nine-year-old on earth. She achieved every single position, from half cobra to downward-facing dog.

The session ended with the room grapevining—an aerobic maneuver akin to line dancing—to Tom Jones's "It's Not Unusual," requested by the usual suspect. When the song ended, everyone cheered and clapped, then began a slow exodus toward the door.

Rose and I rejoined Mary, Blackjack, and Grub in the common room.

"These two sure have a good time together," said Mary, nodding at my brother and Blackjack, who sat side by side, perusing one of Grub's homemade maps. "He's such a creative kid, must run in the family! I think your Sunday surprises are so clever, Zeus. What's lined up next?"

"Well, it's a surprise. I can't say."

"Come on, no hint?" asked Rose with a "pretty please with sugar on top" face that nearly crumbled my resolve.

"Kailangan kong umihi!" declared Blackjack.

Rose and I shared a look, wondering what he'd said.

"I believe Sergeant Blackjack needs to use the restroom," explained Mary.

"Take me to my bunk, nurse," said Blackjack to Mary. He straightened in his chair, head held high, chin up.

"I'll provide cover fire," said Grub, diving behind the wheelchair.

"We have to get going, Private," I said. "I think Mary can cover him." I nodded at Mary, knowing she'd play along.

Mary looked down at Grub and in her best army voice said, "I've got this watch. At ease, Private."

"Ten four," said Grub, followed by a click of his heels and a quick salute.

On Sunday, I woke up feeling one part excited, one part exhilarated, and ninety-eight parts sick to my stomach. A big day lay ahead. Rose and I had planned to meet at World Peas Café at one o'clock. From there we'd make the short walk to the Beauty Saloon—owned and operated by Axl and Novie's mom, Crash. Every Sunday afternoon in the summer, Crash hosted an Open Mic event on the patio of her bar-salon establishment.

For weeks Rose had been asking me to play my guitar for her, but I'd never had the nerve. I mean, Rose was an amazing musician, and I only knew how to strum some basic chords. The thought of her watching me fumble my way through a whole song made me wince every time she brought it up. But she'd kept insisting, so I finally caved.

Every day the past week, after visiting Hilltop, I'd spent a half hour with Dylan learning a song for Rose, one I knew she'd love. After I'd told Dylan the story, he'd not only promised to help but somehow had convinced me to surprise Rose by dedicating it to her at the Open Mic. Dylan would accompany on his guitar. I wasn't brave enough to actually sing it, but I had most of the chords down (and there were a lot of them), with Dylan's reassurance that he'd cover for me if I got lost. Dylan was bringing a guitar for me to borrow—a *real* guitar, not my garage-sale model—and Axl and Novie promised to be there for moral support as well.

Sunday afternoon Rose arrived at the café looking beautiful as ever, and I let her know it.

"I'm so excited!" she said, clasping her hands under her chin and bouncing up and down as if invisible hands held her shoulders, restraining her from jumping.

"Me too," I replied, feigning confidence I didn't feel.

"You have big shoes to fill, Mr. Gunderson. Going to be hard to top last week's psychic adventure."

"Trust me, Miss Santos," I said, throwing my arm around her shoulder, "you're going to love it."

We walked down the street, her leaning into me. As we got closer to Crash's place, we began to hear the muffled sounds of singing and acoustic guitar accompaniment. The rush returned: a mix of adrenaline and stomach cramps.

As we neared the fenced-in patio of the Beauty Saloon, my friends spotted us and greeted us with a collective "Wooo!" Relieved to see them already there, I released Rose from my grasp and sped up my pace to greet my friends.

"What's up, guys!" I shouted, walking toward the fence, which was made of black vertical bars topped with spade-shaped spears to deter after-hours patio furniture thievery.

"The Zeus is loose!" said Axl, coming to greet me at the fence. We shook hands between two iron bars.

"What's up, man?" I said.

"Good to see you, man," said Dylan.

"Hey, what's up?" I replied.

"What's happening, Zeus?" said Novie from a patio chair.

"What's up, Novie?" I said, realizing I'd said "what's up" four times, four ways.

"Aren't you going to introduce us?" asked Dylan, referring to Rose.

"Yeah, man, I—" I turned to introduce Rose only to find that she still stood ten feet behind me. "What are you doing back there, come meet these guys," I said, waving her over.

Rose hesitated, then slowly approached. She stuck her hand through alternating gaps in the fence, shaking each of theirs.

"Come on in, find a seat," said Novie.

I was starting to walk toward the entrance when Rose grabbed my hand and gave it a little tug. She leaned toward my ear. "Zeus, should we be here? This is a *bar*; we're underage. I don't want to get in trouble."

I gave her a look that I thought said, "Don't worry, I got this," but might have missed the mark since she still looked skeptical.

Earlier in the week I had voiced the same concern as hers, regarding teenagers at a bar. Axl and Novie had reassured me though, reminding me their mom owned the place. We weren't allowed inside, but the patio was family friendly. And a local cop apparently frequented the Open Mic circuit, and welcomed any audience: young, old, or underage. It turned out he currently presided over the patio, performing a cringe-worthy version of Tom Petty's "American Girl."

As we walked to find a seat, I sang the chorus in Rose's ear:

"Oh yeah, all right, take it easy baby, make it last all night (make it last all night!)." Dylan motioned for us to sit at the empty chairs at their table. Rose and I sat next to Dylan, across from Axl and Novie.

For the next hour, waves of anxious anticipation washed over me. Rose flashed me a quick smile every time I turned to check on her, though she hardly spoke. *Just being shy,* I thought. I kept imagining her heart melting as she watched me play, especially after I dedicated the song to her. I spent most of the time joking around with Dylan, Axl, and Novie.

The cop finally finished his set.

I felt my heart palpitate.

My big moment.

My musical debut.

Dylan and I shared a look that said, "Here we go." Just as we began to stand and head to the stage area, Rose scooted her chair back and stood herself.

I looked at her and cocked my head to the side, like a dog.

"I think I'm going to head home," she said, forcing a smile.

I cocked my head to the other side. "What are you talking about?" I asked, sounding a bit more annoyed than intended.

"I . . . I need to help my mom with something," she replied, still trying to hold a smile.

Inside I deflated, heartbroken. Rose was bailing on me.

All that buildup for *this?*

"Come on, just one more song!" said Dylan, doing his best to help out.

I slumped my shoulders and looked at Rose. "Stay for one more?"

Rose blinked slowly and took a breath. "I need to go."

I felt like I was going to be sick. I had a dozen different questions I wanted to ask her, but I just stood there with my mouth open. What the hell was she doing? I glanced at the stage. Someone else had already walked up with their gear.

Well, screw it, I thought. *The whole thing's ruined.*

"Fine. See you later," I said, sitting back down.

Rose looked like she wanted to say something. I waited for her to speak, but she turned and walked away.

TWENTY-ONE

THE NEXT DAY WAS MONDAY, THE THIRD OF JULY, WHICH MEANT FIRE-works would be shot over the river the following night. American flags commemorating the occasion waved from every available pole. It was a balmy ninety-six degrees with eighty-two percent humidity. The low air in my bike tires didn't help the situation, nor did Grub's sweaty hands digging into my shoulders. I ped-aled us across the bridge past the spot where Rose and I had had our first kiss. I glanced at it miserably.

I was still baffled over Rose's sudden departure from the Open Mic. Dylan and I never even ended up playing the song we'd worked on. What was the point? Learning and practicing the song all week meant nothing without Rose there. And what was up with her being so quiet the whole time? I defended her after she left, telling my friends she was just shy. But seriously.

She couldn't have stayed fifteen minutes longer?

My plan was to quickly stop at Hilltop and let Grub see his old pal Blackjack. Then I'd talk to Rose to see what happened yesterday and apologize if I had to. Though I still wasn't sure what I'd done wrong.

But when we approached the common room, the grand piano sat silent, its keyboard covered. *Am I too late?* I wondered, checking the wall clock: two thirty. *Rose should be here.* I spotted Mary and Blackjack across the room.

Grub and I wove through the tables.

Mary stood by a tall window, staring out at the property grounds. Blackjack sat hunched beside her, gazing blankly at the floor. I started to get a sick feeling, like I was about to receive some awful news.

"Mary," I said.

As she turned, a nanosecond passed before she seemed to recognize me. Finally, a forced smile appeared.

Oh God. Something terrible has happened.

Mary read my expression, which was wide-eyed and slack-jawed to match my pallor. "Rose isn't feeling well," she said flatly.

My brain scrambled like a microwave full of metal forks set to high.

"She's sick?"

Mary took a slow, deep breath. She shook her head no.

"What's wrong? Is she okay?" I asked, the blood returning to my face.

Mary hesitated again. "She's home. She's had a bad day."

Oh no. I pissed Rose off and she told her mom and now her mom's pissed at me and I'm standing here like a jackass. I had to think fast. I needed to see Rose.

"I'll go see her, I'll make things right," I blurted.

Mary shook her head. "That's nice of you, Zeus, but I don't think she wants company today."

Shit. This is not good. I felt my pulse increasing. "I need to see her. It's my fault, I'll fix it."

"There's nothing to fix, Zeus. I think she wants to be alone."

This is bad. Did I say something I don't remember? What did I do? "No, trust me, I can make this better. I'll go there right now."

Mary considered me a moment. "I'm not sure that's the best idea."

"I have to," I said. "Please."

Mary sighed. "Well, I suppose it should be Rose telling you, not me. But Zeus . . ."

"Yeah?"

"She's under a lot of stress. Keep that in mind."

"Of course," I said. Then I motioned to Grub, who had been hiding behind my legs. "Would you mind keeping an eye on him?"

For the first time since we arrived, Mary genuinely smiled. "Of course not."

Grub left the safety of my legs and approached Blackjack, poking him in the shoulder. Blackjack slowly turned and studied my brother with vacant eyes. "Who are you?"

Grub blanched as Mary and I exchanged a worried look over his head.

Blackjack squinted closer at Grub. "Do I know you?"

Grub took a cautious step forward. "Private Grub, sir?" he said.

Blackjack slowly blinked a few times, then his face broke into a smile. "Of course you are. What took you so long, Private? I have a new top-secret mission to discuss with you."

"I'm at your command," said Grub with a salute.

I raised my eyebrows at Mary in question and she nodded in response. "Go on," she mouthed.

Mary and Rose's apartment was less than a mile from Hilltop, so I had a short ride to prepare my thoughts. As I pumped the bike pedals through the thick heat, I rehearsed various conversations in my head, uncertain about what to expect.

I was worried.

Had I screwed up our entire relationship in one fell swoop?

I turned into their ground-level apartment complex, which formed a U shape around a blacktop parking lot. I propped the bike on its kickstand and walked up the short sidewalk to the front door. The curtains had been drawn, the mailbox lid flipped open wide, empty. I paused, deliberating whether to ring the doorbell or knock.

I knocked.

I heard movement inside and wondered if my fish-eyed profile was being viewed through the peephole. I heard the locks turn.

Deep breath.

Here we go.

The door opened, and Rose stood before me in yoga pants and a T-shirt. Her hair was tied back in a messy ponytail. She wore no makeup, and her face was blotchy red, eyes swollen from crying.

I hadn't prepared for crying.

"Hi," she said in a soft voice. She looked surprised to see me.

"Hi," I said back, trying to match her tone. "What's wrong?" I asked.

She shook her head. "Nothing."

Unconvinced, I asked again. "No, tell me. What's wrong?"

She shook her head again, faster. "It's nothing."

"Obviously it's something," I said. "What is it? Is it me? Something I said yesterday?"

Rose gave the slightest hint of an eye roll. "Zeus, I'm just not ready to talk about it yet."

"Can I come in at least?"

"Fine, come in. But it's not you." She opened the door all the way, and I walked into the living room.

"What is it then?"

Rose crossed her arms. "Are you seriously going to make me talk about this? I've told you like three times I don't want to."

I decided to take the bull by the horns. "Okay, I was kind of a jerk yesterday. I should have walked you out. I should have—"

"Zeus, this isn't about yesterday."

"Well, what then? Tell me."

Rose's mouth tightened, and her eyes welled with tears. "Fine. Since you won't let it go, I'll tell you. I found out that I can't go to the Manhattan Music Conservatory. The scholarship fell through," she said, her voice catching, "and now I'm stuck here in this stupid town."

Those last words felt like a knife wound to my side. "Stuck here? You mean stuck here with *me*?"

Rose shut her eyes and took a deep breath. "Are you even listening? No scholarship. No New York. No music school."

I thought for a moment, remembering how Mary had said Rose was under a lot of stress. "Is that why you were acting so weird yesterday at the Open Mic?"

Rose moved her head back, as if dodging an invisible bee. "Actually, I just got the letter this morning. You don't even care, do you?"

"What are you talking about? Of course I care." I felt my pulse increase. She had *no idea* how much I cared—I cared about her more than anything! I'd spent an entire week learning a song for her, risking it all, ready to embarrass myself in front of a crowd. For her!

Rose looked at a spot above my shoulder. "Well, it doesn't feel like it."

"How do you think it made me feel when you left the Open Mic yesterday?"

Rose's eyes flashed back to mine. "You know what? Let's talk about yesterday some other time, okay?"

Apparently, I couldn't say anything right. "So we can't talk about this, we can't talk about that, and I don't care about how you feel. Does that sum it all up?"

The tears returned to her eyes. "I told you I wasn't ready to talk about this."

"Rose—"

"Maybe you should go." Rose opened the door.

I left.

TWENTY-TWO

I'D BEEN WATCHING THE CEILING FAN SPIN ALL MORNING, LISTENING to the *clickity-clack* of its off-kilter rotation. I kept replaying the fight in my head, analyzing everything I could remember. But her last words kept thundering back to me: *Maybe you should go.*

And that look on her face . . .

I finally summoned the energy to stand on my bed and pull the chain to change the speed setting, only to have it snap off in my hand and send me falling into the headboard.

Great, stuck on high forever, I thought. *What else can I break?*

I'd single-handedly ruined the only relationship I'd ever had. With the only girl I'd ever wanted. She'd received terrible news, and instead of being there for her, I'd made everything worse. And now she probably hated me. She *definitely* hated me. She'd kicked me out of her house.

I hadn't eaten, I'd barely slept, and I'd hardly left my room except to answer a few calls of nature. I still wore my clothes from yesterday, which reeked of sweat and failure. If a color described my mood, it'd be dull gray; a sound, a muted trumpet going *wah-wah-waaaaah*. I tried strumming my guitar for a while, but all that came out was off-key dissonance.

Fortunately, the café was closed for the Fourth of July, so I didn't have to worry about making deliveries. That gave me plenty of time to let my thoughts wander and feel sorry for myself. Every time Rose came to mind, I felt slightly ill. Of course, everything made me think of Rose.

Spider plant by the window: *Plant. Flower. Rose*

Guitar leaning against the door: *Guitar. Piano. Rose.*

Dirty socks on the floor: *Rose has feet. Rose.*

I was trying to sleep again when I heard a soft knock on my door. I rolled over into my pillow and grunted. Another knock. I grunted louder. A third knock. I lifted my head and grunted unmistakably at the door.

"Zeus, can I come in?" said Mom.

"*Gaarrg,*" I replied.

"Is that a yes?"

"*Mmmph.*" I pulled the pillow over my head. I heard the door open.

"Honey, there's some sandwiches in the kitchen if you're hungry."

"Mrrraamph," I said into the mattress. I felt the bed shift slightly as she sat next to me. *"Mrrraamph,"* I repeated. I felt her hand on my foot. I brought my leg toward me, which left me looking like a splayed-out frog on its belly.

"Zeus, what's wrong, sweetie?"

"Errrmm," I replied. She placed her hand on my foot again. Short of dislocating my hip, I'd run out of room, so I begrudgingly received her consolation.

"You haven't left your room since you got home yesterday."

"Mmmhmm."

"Zeus, can you at least look at me?"

I slowly removed the pillow from my head and rolled over. Mom reached out and gently brushed the hair from my forehead with her fingertips. Instantly, her touch reminded me of being sick when I was younger, when she'd magically appear in the middle of the night to soothe me and lie with me until I fell back asleep. The sixteen-year-old part of me wanted to swat her hand away. The six-year-old part of me wanted to curl up in her lap.

I felt my eyes tickle and burn as my brain sent signals to my tear ducts to activate. I didn't want to cry in front of my mom, I really didn't. Why'd she have to go and touch me? Dammit.

"It's okay," she said. And suddenly, it was. She put her arms around me and held me tight. We both cried—me out of self-pity for being an asshole; her, I assumed, for seeing me suffer.

After regaining my composure, I told her everything. I told her how miserable I'd been after moving to Buffalo Falls, how lonely and out of place I'd felt. And then how I'd met Rose, how she'd made everything better and more fun when I was with her. I told her about the polka dancing, the movie at Hilltop, the psychic—all of it—and how they'd been the best days of my life. And then I told her about the Open Mic and Rose's scholarship news, and how I'd screwed it all up, and how Rose told me to leave, and how she probably never wanted to see me again.

Mom sat cross-legged at the end of my bed listening to the whole thing, nodding when appropriate, and making soft *mmm*s and *mm-hmm*s when needed.

When I reached the end, she let everything sink in before speaking.

"Opening your heart to people can sometimes be painful. But it's a beautiful thing, Zeus, it really is."

"It doesn't feel beautiful."

"Not always, no. But it means you *have* a heart, son. And that you care about someone enough for it to hurt. I'm sure Rose is feeling the same way you are right now. Worse, maybe."

I remembered the look on Rose's face when she told me she wasn't getting into the conservatory. She'd felt bad enough receiving the news, then on top of it, I'd showed up and acted like a complete jerk. I couldn't believe I'd been so stupid. What was I thinking?

"Now, are you ready for some tough love?"

I wasn't.

"Sure," I said.

"You've been a little self-involved this summer."

I felt my stomach sink. "Really?"

"And it's okay—you're sixteen. You're a *teenager*. You're supposed to go out and make mistakes and have fun. These are all little life lessons; you learn from them or you don't. But if you choose to learn from them, you become a better person, which will make you a better *man*."

I looked at my mom and realized how little I'd seen of her lately. We'd always been close—after all, it was just the two of us those first eight years before Grub came along. I saw the crow's-feet at the corners of her eyes, and the gray that now highlighted her brown hair. Where had the time gone? Had I been a jerk to her, too? *God, I have, haven't I?*

"How have *you* been?" I asked, trying to summarize my thoughts.

Mom looked surprised by the question, which was enough to let me know it had been too long since I'd asked.

"If we're being honest here, I'm a bit worried," she said.

"About what?"

"Well, about you, for one. About your brother. About other things."

"Like what, the café?"

Mom paused, then nodded.

I'd feared this news for a while, though I'd tried to ignore the signs. "Is it bad?" I asked.

"Hard to say at this point. When I was waitressing, as much as I disliked it, the money was steady. Still, I thought: my own business, small town, cheaper rent, lower cost of living, no problem. But it's been a lot harder converting people from cheeseburgers to tofu than I thought it would be. May have to rethink things."

I felt my stomach drop again. "Rethink things? What does that mean?"

"I'm not sure. It could mean changing the menu. It could mean shutting down and finding a new job here. Or it could mean moving back to Chicago and taking my old job back."

Moving back to Chicago. The words I'd once longed to hear now echoed in my head like a death sentence . . . the death of my relationship with Rose, or whatever was left of it.

Mom continued. "And I haven't even begun to start paying back the money your aunt Willow loaned me. I'm not sure how I ever will at this point."

I watched the ceiling fan spin for a minute before responding. "Is that why we haven't been up to see her?" Every summer for as long as I could remember, we spent a week at Aunt Willow's cottage in Wisconsin. I'd been so preoccupied with Rose, I'd nearly forgotten about it.

Mom sighed. "No, of course not. You know your aunt, she's been nothing but supportive. We'll try to make it up there later this summer. Manny's been asking about it, too. I just can't afford to close the café right now. I need every customer I can get." She saw the look on my face. "Don't worry, sweetie, there's still time to turn this ship around."

I changed the subject slightly. "You said you're worried about me."

"That's my job, I'm your mom. All I want is for you to be happy and healthy. Right now, you're neither. You're depressed, heartbroken, and malnourished. Have a sandwich. Take a shower. You smell." She winked.

I laughed. "It gets worse," I said. "I have a spiritual blockage."

"Yes, I heard. That's unfortunate."

"I need to surround myself in white light to keep the bad spirits away." I did the lasso motion above my head, like Mo had.

"Well, save some white light for the rest of us." She lay down next to me. We listened to the rattle of the ceiling fan until I fell asleep. When I woke, she was gone.

Our apartment was only a few blocks from the river, so that night the three of us ventured out to watch the fireworks. We found a spot with a clear view, sitting on some old train tracks away from the crowd.

"One last little piece of advice," Mom said, turning to me. "You should apologize to Rose. It will mean a lot. Whatever ends up happening—and who knows what will happen—it's

179

the right thing to do."

She was right. I'd apologize tomorrow. "I will," I said.

"Don't worry," said Grub, sliding a foot back and forth through the gravel. "Blackjack has a plan."

Mom and I shared a look. Then she reached down and ruffled his hair.

Under the starry sky, gunpowder missiles flashed into giant Epcot spheres with sizzling spider legs. I felt the cannon explosions reverberate in my chest cavity. As I looked at my mother and brother bathed in white light, I thought I understood what the psychic meant.

TWENTY-THREE

THE NEXT MORNING, I GOT UP EARLY TO HELP MOM CLEAN THE CAFÉ. IT wouldn't solve the problems she faced, but I hoped it would at least ease her workload. It also gave me time to consider my options. I knew Rose would be at Hilltop at noon, but I couldn't wait that long. I'd been lying in bed since before dawn rehearsing my apology. I couldn't show up at the nursing home and apologize in front of everyone though—what if she didn't accept my apology? Stormed off? Wasn't there? What if I made things worse? They all seemed realistic, if not likely, possibilities.

No, if I wanted to apologize to Rose it would have to be somewhere private.

In the café kitchen, Mom sang to herself while washing vegetables. The doors wouldn't open to the public for another hour.

The aroma of dark, organic coffee brewing smelled tempting, but caffeine seemed like a bad idea. I didn't need to end up chattering like a wind-up set of teeth.

Across from me, Grub drew a map. I leaned forward to take a look. He'd drawn a building next to a small battlefield. Little trees and bushes lined the field's perimeter, and Xs had been circled at various locations, like a treasure map. A big dog that looked suspiciously like Agatha stood guard.

For a brief moment, I wished I were eight years old again, lost in my own imagination. No time for wishful thinking though; time for action. Waiting until the afternoon—even if I could get Rose away from the crowd at Hilltop—was out of the question. Showing up at Rose's house without warning also seemed like a bad idea.

That left one option.

I burst through the kitchen door, making Mom jump like she'd been tased.

"Mom, can I use the phone? Real quick. One text."

"Sure thing," she replied, pulling it out of her back pocket. A gold corona of light shone around it as if she were unsheathing Excalibur.

Okay, not really. But I'd gone over a month without using it for the most part, as "just a week or two" had turned into "indefinitely."

Before handing it to me, she said, "I want you to know

how much I appreciate you loaning me this. It's been a lifesaver. Thank you."

Part of me wanted to say, "What choice did I have?" The other part knew better.

"No problem," I said. Truthfully, it had been liberating to be phoneless. After the post-phonum depression and phantom-limb feeling went away, it hadn't been a big deal at all.

I returned to the booth and scrolled through my contact list until I came to Rose Santos. I stared at the number with trepidation before opening a text message. The cursor blinked back at me, daring me to type. I began a message, then deleted it. Another, deleted it. A third, deleted it.

Stop it, I told myself. *Just keep it simple.*

I typed a message, shut my eyes, and hit send. I hovered over the phone for several minutes in anticipation, praying for a response. I'd typed: So sorry about the other day. Need to see you.

A minute passed by.

Another.

When the phone finally dinged I nearly fell out of the booth. Need to see you too. :)

I breathed a sigh of relief. She needed to see me too, and had even added a smiley. Best. Smiley. Ever. I replied and told her to sit tight because I'd be there in twenty minutes.

I gave the phone back to Mom and asked her if I could have two triple chocolate brownies and two coffees to go. She smiled and said, "I see I've taught you well." I bagged everything up, promised I'd be back for Grub soon, and headed out.

Before crossing the bridge, I stopped at home to grab one more last-minute item.

Nineteen minutes later, I stood in front of Rose's door catching my breath. It felt like weeks had passed since we'd seen each other, even though it had only been two days. My heart pounded in my chest as if trying to escape. I breathed deeply to compose myself. I knocked. A moment later the door opened and Rose stood before me.

I launched into an incoherent monologue like a pull-string doll with a faulty speech setting. While I'm pretty sure I blacked out for most of it, I think it went something like:

"Rose I'm so sorry about the other day I was a total jerk I can't believe I said those things to you I should have been more understanding of your situation I'm sorry you didn't get into the school and I'm sorry I didn't pay attention to you at the Open Mic I just had to make new friends because I thought you'd be leaving at the end of the summer and I need to have some friends after you're gone I'm so sorry I'm a jerk I understand if you never want to see me again but I just had to apologize I brought you a present."

I held out the box containing the two brownies and the tray with the coffees. "I'm sorry," I said again.

Rose took the peace offering. "I'm sorry, too," she said softly.

"You are? Thanks." I wondered if thanking her for a mutual apology was weird.

We stood in uncomfortable silence for a moment.

"What is it?" she asked, peeking inside the box.

"It's a brownie," I said, experiencing intense déjà vu.

Rose's mouth hinted at a smile. "Turn That Frownie Upside Brownie?"

"That's the one," I replied. "And cold coffee. Sorry it's only half-full, the rest of it is on the sidewalk between here and downtown."

"It's okay, I'll go lick it up later."

"I'm sorry," I said.

"Don't be, the dirt adds flavor and texture."

I grinned, then shoved my hands in my pockets. "About the other day, I mean. I can't believe I said those things to you, Rose. I was totally inconsiderate. Can you forgive me?"

"It's okay, I was really emotional. I shouldn't have told you to leave."

We stood in the doorway. My eyes darted around, trying to find anything to settle on. I don't think either of us had prepared for what to say next. Rose finally broke the silence. "Come on in."

Relief—decidedly the best of all feelings—flowed through my veins. I could breathe again; think again.

Inside, Rose sat on a couch and I on a wooden chair.

I noticed a stack of library books on the coffee table between us. I read the titles: *Museums of New York City*; *So Now You Live in NYC, What Next?*; *From Cave Paintings to Modernism: Art*

History; *The Impressionists*; and on top, *Sacré Bleu: A Comedy d'Art.*

"Have you read all of those?" I asked, pointing to the stack.

Rose looked at the books the way one might consider a pair of dirty underwear. "Not yet," she said. "I started to, you know, before I found out . . ."

. . . *that you're not going to New York City*, my brain finished her sentence.

"You were really looking forward to going, weren't you?" I said.

She nodded.

"There's always college, right?"

She nodded again, then looked up at me. "I shouldn't have said that I'll be stuck in this town. At least I'll have you here."

I began to speak, but my voice caught in my throat. My mom's words came thundering back to haunt me: *It could mean changing the menu. It could mean shutting down and finding a new job here. Or it could mean moving back to Chicago and taking my old job back.*

"What's wrong?" Rose asked.

"Nothing," I replied.

She raised an eyebrow and smirked at me. "Do we want to play that game again?"

She was right. "Well, it might be nothing, it might not. Too soon to tell. I guess the café is struggling a bit. My mom mentioned . . . It's possible we may have to move back to Chicago." I'd been looking at the floor while speaking but glanced up to see Rose's reaction. She was looking at the floor as well, nodding her head. Then she snorted and laughed.

"What?" I said.

Rose laughed harder. "It's kind of funny when you think about it."

"It is?"

"I find out I'm staying here, and now *you* may be the one leaving. It's probably your spiritual blockage messing everything up."

I laughed too. "Yeah, I still need to work on that."

"So what do we do?" she asked.

I thought for a moment. "Well, maybe it's like Letty says: 'Enjoy today, you might be dead tomorrow.'"

"She might be onto something," Rose said, "though it's a tad morbid."

"Maybe we could just leave it at 'enjoy today.'"

"Deal."

"Shake on it?"

We shook hands, and then Rose pulled out a brownie and offered the other one to me. She took a bite, and her eyes rolled back in her head, like a shark gorging on a hapless surfer. "I'm telling you," she said as specks of brownie went flying, "this is the best item on the menu, hands down."

"I think you're right."

"If your mom opened a bakery, I'd be there every day." Rose finished the brownie and chased it down with a swig of cold coffee. "Zeus, I should have let you know what I was thinking at that Open Mic thing. It was just . . . I felt so uncomfortable and didn't want to be there. I thought our Sundays were supposed to be about you and me, and I felt like you were ignoring me for your friends . . . like it wasn't about us anymore, it was about you and them. I'm really sorry. I shouldn't have left."

I shook my head at the irony, at myself for not seeing it before now. "The thing is, Rose, the Open Mic *was* all about us."

Rose looked confused. "Really? How?"

"I was going to play you a song. But all I could think about was how nervous I felt. I should have realized how uncomfortable it would be for you. I'm the one who's sorry."

Rose's eyes flew open. "You were going to play me a song?"

"Yeah," I said softly.

"Zeus, I feel horrible now!"

"Don't," I said. "I should have planned it better. It was my fault. I never should have done it there, in front of everyone. The song was meant to be for you, anyway, not a bunch of Beauty Saloon regulars."

"What song were you going to play?"

"Do you still want to hear it?"

"Of course I do!"

knew you'd figure it out!"

It was the Beatles song Rose had played the first time I'd seen her at Hilltop. The melody had haunted me ever since that afternoon, the wordless soundtrack to my summer with Rose. "Sorry it took me so long."

"Worth the wait," she said. "Thank you. That was perfect."

It had been far from perfect.

But mission accomplished.

TWENTY-FOUR

THOUGH I HADN'T REALIZED IT AT THE TIME, A SEED HAD BEEN PLANTED in my head while at Rose's house. Over the next few weeks, it germinated, took root, and grew into a fully formed idea—possibly my best Sunday surprise yet. Meanwhile, I had a few other Sundays to fill.

The week after the Open Mic, I took Rose to the local farmers' market. I'd learned from Mom that it was a weekly occurrence held on a side street near the park downtown. I'd joked to Rose that it would probably be a handful of locals selling corn and beans out of their pickup trucks, but it was nothing of the sort. Well, there *were* people selling fresh-picked fruits and vegetables from their flatbeds, but there was so much more.

One family sold handmade soaps and candles. A husband-and-wife team displayed glazed pottery and blown-glass art. At another tent, a man offered venison, duck, geese, and free-range chicken from an assortment of large coolers. Other vendors touted organic cheeses, wild mushrooms, flowers, and coffee beans. After spending nearly an hour there, Rose walked away with a shiny jeweled bracelet made from guitar strings, and I picked up fresh-baked bread, homemade peanut butter, and rhubarb strawberry jam, which made for some killer sandwiches afterward.

The next week Dylan helped by lending me an old canoe his parents had in the garage. It looked ridiculous strapped to the top of the Lego as we drove to the park. Then again, it didn't look a whole lot better in the water, like a piece of driftwood in need of a paint job. But Rose was a good sport, as usual, and we did our best not to capsize our borrowed vessel in the Stone River. We only tipped once, which we considered a grand success.

Finally, the big day came. My biggest surprise yet.

Hilltop Nursing Home's annual field trip fell on the third Sunday of July. The destination: Wrigley Field, home of the Chicago Cubs. After getting the green light from Candy, Mom, and Mary, I'd asked Rose to go, and she'd agreed. Neither of us were huge baseball fans, but that didn't matter. If all went according to plan, we'd never step foot inside Wrigley Field.

Outside of Hilltop, the bus awaited us. It sat twenty people legally and fifteen comfortably. Final count: thirteen residents, four volunteers, three personal nurses, two turtledoves, and a partridge in a pear tree.

Mary and Blackjack had stayed behind—he'd had a bad couple of weeks, unable to leave his room. Grub roamed the hallways by himself on whatever "top-secret mission" Blackjack had tasked him with. My little brother had become a fixture by then at Hilltop, much as he was in our old Chicago neighborhood. The residents and staff doted on him, plying him with treats and allowing him free rein throughout the nursing home. Grub still steered clear of Missy Stouffer, though, as we all did.

Fortunately, she'd decided to skip the baseball game, too.

Once some of the less physically able residents had been seated, Rose and I climbed aboard. The bus did not have typical rows like a school bus, but cushioned bench seating around the perimeter, facing inward. Rose and I sat next to each other in the middle across from Letty and the Bettys. Next to us, Lucille and George Larsen loudly discussed her missing wedding ring.

"It was on the nightstand," said Lucille.

George craned his ear toward her. "You had a one-night stand?"

"Night. Stand."

"Stan? Who's Stan?"

Lucille held up her hand for her beloved to see.

"Where's your wedding ring?"

Candy's bubbly voice came through an intercom system overhead. "Welcome aboard, ladies and gentleman. Our estimated departure time is T minus thirty seconds. It is currently a sunny, eighty-degree day in Chicago. Our cruising speed will be roughly seventy miles per hour, which should have us arriving at our destination at approximately twelve thirty, Central Standard Time. Please fasten your seat belts, and enjoy the ride."

The diesel engine rumbled, and everyone cheered as the brass intro to Dean Martin's "Ain't That a Kick in the Head?" came through the speakers. Letty threw her arms in the air and danced in her seat. She wore a red-and-blue Cubs wind suit and all-white sneakers, and topped the ensemble with matching Cubs earrings and blackout sunglasses fit for viewing an atomic blast.

As we merged onto the interstate, I put my arm around Rose and she leaned into me. We could have been driving to Canada for all I cared. Lucille and George had already fallen asleep next to us, but Letty, the Bettys, and the rest of the Hilltoppers sang and swayed to the music. I rested my head on Rose's and watched the cornfields fly by. Rose pushed open my free hand and began tracing the lines on my palm.

"That line there," she said. "I think that means today will be a good day."

"I think you're psychic," I replied.

I shut my eyes and listened to Dean Martin and the steady hum of the engine.

I must have drifted off to sleep, for when I opened my eyes, the Chicago skyline projected from the horizon in the distance. Rose's head lay under my arm, on my chest. Our hands had become sweaty from holding them together so long.

"Rose," I whispered. "You asleep?"

"Nope," she replied, muffled by my shirt. "You were though. I was trapped under your arm. Also, you snore."

"I do?"

"Like a buzz saw."

I yawned and stretched my neck. "Sorry about that." I felt slightly embarrassed, but at the same time I didn't mind. I didn't care what she knew about me.

"It's okay. I like the way you snore," Rose said, smiling up at me. "You make cute choking sounds." I tried to give her shoulder a squeeze, but my arm had gone to pins and needles, so I just groped her arm with a lifeless hand. The music was off now and many others had fallen asleep as well.

Across from us, Letty held a Cubs pennant flag in one hand, looking perplexed. "What the hell happened? I'm ready to party," she said.

Rose and I laughed.

"You know what this bus needs?" I asked Letty.

She cocked her head to the side and raised an eyebrow.

"Tom Jones," I said.

Letty's eyes lit up. "If I wasn't strapped to this seat, I'd come over there and kiss you." Then, to Candy, who sat behind the bus driver, "You hear that, Candy Apple? My personal volunteer would like some Tom Jones!"

Candy shook her head with a grin, then scrolled through her phone's playlist. A minute later, "Help Yourself" roared through the speakers, and one by one, the bus revived as Mr. Jones invited us to help ourselves to his heart, arms, lips, and love.

The skyline grew larger on the horizon. Rose had told me she'd only been to Chicago a couple times, and it had been years since her last visit. I was excited to show her the city, but more excited for the other surprise that lay in store for her.

We passed an exit near Midway Airport, and I pointed. "That's the exit we'd take to get to my old house," I said.

Rose craned her neck to see out the window. "It must have been so different growing up here compared to Buffalo Falls."

You can say that again, I thought. Something felt odd though. I figured driving into Chicago would feel like a homecoming of sorts—I hadn't been back since we'd moved. But it felt different. *I* felt different. I'd grown used to Buffalo Falls. The sound of insects at night had become a comfort rather than an annoyance, and the slower pace felt more familiar now than this four-lane expressway. As for my old friends, I still texted them now and then, but it wasn't the same. We'd all moved on, I guess. *I'd* moved on.

An unsettling feeling came over me as I remembered the possibility of moving back. But then I remembered our new motto: *Enjoy today.*

The expressway became Lake Shore Drive. Lake Michigan appeared before us, looking as blue and expansive as any ocean. Sailboats cut white wakes through the water beyond a harbor full of yachts, their white hulls shining in the sun. Overhead, a plane flew by with a message trailing behind it too small to read. Turning north, we drove by McCormick Place, then Soldier Field, home of the Chicago Bears. Passing Millennium Park, I told Rose about how Mom used to take me and Grub there for picnics and free music on the weekends.

Farther north, the buildings became smaller and less cramped together. We turned off the Addison exit toward Wrigley Field, and my heart sped up with excitement. As the stadium came into view, Letty led the bus through "Take Me Out to the Ball Game."

"A-one, a-two, a-three . . . *Take me out to the ball game, take me out with the crowd!*" Letty sang.

A few simply listened, George Larsen snored, but most of the bus joined in and belted out the rest of the song.

"*For it's ONE! TWO! THREE strikes you're out at the old ball game!*" Letty finished with a heroic fist in the air.

"Play ball!" someone shouted.

"Go, Cubbies!" shouted another.

The bus parked in a handicapped zone in front of the stadium, where dozens of people milled about beneath the bright red Wrigley Field sign. Across the marquee, the golden words *Welcome Hilltop Residents* scrolled by. Rose and I waited for everyone to exit the bus, then joined them on the sidewalk and made our way to the gates. Letty was first in line, followed by the Bettys. When Letty reached the checkpoint, she held her arms in the air.

"Go ahead and pat me down, big fella. I ain't scared. I might even like it," she said to the man with the ticket scanner.

"That's right, she ain't scared," said Betty.

"Go on, pat her down!" said the other Betty. And then all three cackled and laughed.

Rose and I were last in line. Once the others had passed the ticket and security check, I took a deep breath. Candy and I made eye contact and she winked at me. I winked back.

"My first major league baseball game," said Rose, smiling up at the stadium.

"Actually, that will have to wait."

Rose whipped her head around at me. "What?"

I raised my eyebrows at her. "Follow me."

I took Rose by the hand and we raced across the street. I led her down the block as far as possible from Wrigley Field, for we'd never find a taxi there. We wove between people, around kiosks, and past gated beer gardens. We crossed another street, then another. Cars honked at us. Pigeons scattered into the air as we rounded a corner. We passed hot dog vendors, music stores, and at least seventeen Starbucks. Eventually I stopped, walked to the curb, and looked down the street.

"Where are we going?" Rose asked, breathless from running. "What about the game?"

"Have you forgotten? It's Sunday," I said between breaths. "This is the surprise part!" I flagged a taxi and we slid into the rear seat. "Now, cover your ears." Rose put her hands over her ears and I told the driver where to go. Our heads flew back as he accelerated into traffic, narrowly missing another car.

Rose gripped my arm as we slid across the vinyl seat with every lane change.

"Is the surprise that we make it there alive?" she said under her breath.

"Think of it as a hair-raising adventure."

It took us fifteen minutes to get from Wrigley Field to our destination. We turned onto Michigan Avenue, and our driver pulled over to the curb. I paid him with my tip money, and we stepped into the summer sun.

I took Rose by the hand and led her up a wide staircase flanked by two stone lions.

TWENTY-FIVE

"CHECK THIS OUT!" SAID ROSE AS WE APPROACHED A CHISELED SCULP-
ture of a portly nude fellow. She read the placard aloud. "*Portrait
of Balzac* by Auguste Rodin. I've read about Balzac. He was a
French writer."

"Oh, nice. Hey, let's look at this one," I said, grabbing her
hand and walking toward something else—anything besides a
naked man with a name that made me think of frank and beans,
as Letty would say. Clearly, my art appreciation left much to be
desired.

I'd been to the Art Institute before, but it had been a while.
Fourth-grade field trip. I remembered thinking it was boring
except for the medieval armor room, but today was for Rose,
not me. Even though things had been going great since I'd apol-
ogized and played the song, I still felt the need to make it up to

her. So, having remembered the stack of books about art and museums on her coffee table, I'd been banking on today to blow her away.

We'd only been there ten minutes, and already it had been a huge success.

We stood before the centerpiece of the room, Georges Seurat's *A Sunday Afternoon on La Grande Jatte*. I looked at the massive painting with my arms crossed, nodding thoughtfully. "It's interesting," I said after a while. Those two words summed up my entire understanding of art.

"It's *pointillism,*" said Rose.

"Uh-huh," I said, as if I understood. "It looks like a bunch of dots."

"Right, it's just a bunch of dots up close. But when you step back, you get the whole picture."

We stepped back twenty feet or so to observe, then walked up close again. "Cool," I said. "So what's with the monkey in the corner?"

"Who knows? Maybe Seurat had a monkey fetish. Or maybe he put it there so people would talk about it."

"Like a conversation starter?"

"Right."

"I wonder how many people have stood right here and had this very conversation?"

Rose turned to face me. "Probably just us." She planted a quick kiss on my mouth. I puckered at the air as her face went away. "Too slow," she said, grinning.

We wandered down a long hallway that opened into various rooms on either side. We picked the one that looked the least crowded and walked in. Paintings of naked women and ugly babies lined the walls. We approached one featuring a particularly hideous cherub gazing disdainfully into the middle distance.

"Remember what Mo the psychic said? About you being a painter in a past life?"

"Yeah?"

"You definitely painted this one," I told Rose.

Rose made a face. "You think?"

"Definitely. You were the premier ugly baby painter of your time. People traveled great distances to meet the famous Rose Santos: Ugly Baby Painter Extraordinaire."

Rose tilted her head to the side. "He isn't *that* ugly."

I turned to face her. "Are you kidding me? That kid has a severe appearance deficit."

"This says it's Cupid," said Rose, reading the placard.

"The God of Love? No way. That baby's a poster boy for abstinence," I said.

Rose gave me a slight elbow to the ribs. "Come on, art boy."

We split apart in the next room, where I found myself confronted by a painting of souls entering heaven. A guy in his early twenties appeared next to me, twiddling his curled mustache like a cartoon villain. His hair had been shaved on the sides and left long on top, dyed blue, and wrapped tightly in a bun. Circular, yellow-framed glasses—which I'm not entirely sure had lenses—perched on the end of his nose. Cuffed, skin-tight jeans met worn, leather boots, screaming accessory over necessary. I wanted to remind him it was July.

I glanced down at my own ensemble—T-shirt, shorts, and sandals—and decided it was perfectly sensible and efficient. I also swallowed the realization I was becoming my mom.

I continued to look at the painting, watching hipster dude out of the corner of my eye. He seemed like the type of person whose museum behavior had been groomed and perfected after many long appointments with mirrors. Maybe I could learn something from him. I crossed my arms and rubbed my chin, not having a mustache to twirl myself. I wondered how much time should pass before commenting on the painting, or if I should say anything at all. I tried to think of something profound to offer, perhaps a reference to the meaning of life or the existence of God. On the other hand, maybe I could slink away, unnoticed.

"Your thoughts?" hipster dude asked, nodding toward the painting.

Damn. Don't say it's interesting, don't say it's interesting.

"It's interesting," I said.

He raised an eyebrow and returned his gaze to the painting.

"*Heaven is a place, a place where nothing, nothing ever happens. David Byrne.*"

Don't say cool.

"Cool," I said.

"*Namaste.*" He gave me a slight bow, then walked off, trailed by a breeze of patchouli and pretense.

Rose returned and joined me. "What did that guy say?"

"That nothing ever happens in heaven. Then I think he said something in Spanish."

"Huh. So I say we bail on the Ugly Babies and Naked People Wing."

"Agreed."

We roamed into a long, wide room with display cases of terra-cotta heads, clay pots, and jewelry from Southeast Asia, most of them hundreds if not thousands of years old. Rose loved the Buddhas in particular and told me how her dad had promised to take her to the Philippines someday.

"Of course, that was before he got remarried in May and became insta-dad to three new stepkids," she said with a rueful smile.

"I suppose you'll be wanting *me* to take you to the Philippines now. How many Sundays are left this summer?"

Rose laughed, a sound I loved more than music. "Are you going to ride me there on your bike?"

"Have you seen what these legs can do?" I said, gesturing to my skinny legs as if they were the limbs of Adonis.

Rose shook her head. "Yeah, we wouldn't get far with those bean poles. Maybe we could hitch a ride on a whale."

"Good idea. I could hold on to the blowhole, and you could ride bazooka on the dorsal fin." I shook my head at our exchange. "You know, we have very strange conversations, you and I."

"I know," Rose replied. "That's why I like you."

As we reached the staircase leading down to the lobby, Rose checked her phone for the time and made a pouty face. "We should probably get back to the bus, huh?"

"You're right, we should cruise. Letty's probably behind home plate right now flashing her boobs at the pitcher."

Rose bit back a smile. "It's her ninetieth birthday in a few weeks. She gave me a list of songs to play at her party."

"For what, the male strippers?" I joked.

"Stop!" she said, snorting. "But seriously, we should learn a song to play together."

I chuckled. "Yeah, right."

"Come on, it'll be fun!"

I stopped walking and looked at her. "I'm not that great, Rose. You've heard me play." Obviously, the idea of playing a song with her sounded incredible, but also a bit terrifying. I wasn't sure I could keep up.

"I'll teach you something then. Tom Jones, or Frank Sinatra, or Dean Martin, or whatever Letty wants."

"All right, if you insist. I'm warning you though, I'm very average."

"No, you aren't. You're quite above average." Rose grabbed my hand and interlaced our fingers. "In fact, you're one of the most above-average people I know."

How did she always know the right thing to say? "You're pretty above average yourself, Rose."

We walked down the marble stairs into the lobby, where our path once again crossed with hipster dude's. He walked out of the gift shop carrying a medieval helmet replica under his arm, looking right past me to Rose.

"M'lady," he said, smiling and genuflecting. Then he turned his eyes to me. "Good *day*, sir," he clipped, in a way that felt insulting. As he turned on his heel to walk away, I almost shook my fist and shouted, "May all your hens lay rotten eggs!"

Instead, I just stood there.

"I think I'll dye my hair blue," I said to Rose.

Rose brushed the hair from my forehead, as if consoling a small child. "Aw, you should. It would match your eyes."

We walked back out to the sunshine. I'd forgotten how alive the city felt; it almost had a pulse, almost breathed. Suddenly, it felt good to be back, if only just for an afternoon. I was glad I got to share it with Rose.

I thought back to the painting. "So do *you* believe in heaven?" I asked her as we descended the stairs to the sidewalk.

Rose paused. "Honestly, I don't know. The idea of spending eternity in the clouds where everything is perfect kind of horrifies me. I mean, wouldn't you get sick of it? How would you even know what *perfect* is if every day was exactly the same?"

"True," I replied. "What *is* a perfect day? And compared to what? The perfect yesterday? The perfect tomorrow?"

We walked half a block before either of us spoke again.

"So what would your heaven include if you could choose?" I asked.

Rose thought about it for a minute before answering. "Playing Chopin on piano. Lying on a blanket outside, staring at the stars. My grandmother's hands. Sleeping in on the weekend. The ocean. Poetry. Art. Your mom's brownies," she said with a grin. "What about you? What's your heaven?"

I put my arm around her and pulled her close. "Here. This. Now."

You, I thought.

Eventually we hailed a taxi and made it back to the bus on time. Rose slept on my shoulder the entire ride home. I didn't sleep though.

I couldn't.

Sometimes when a day is perfect, it needs to last just a little while longer.

international calling costs an arm, a leg, and a couple fingers, limiting us to a single, five-minute conversation. Our connection was poor, but I'll try to summarize: (1) Saint Thomas was the most beautiful place in the galaxy; (2) *amazing* didn't begin to describe the great time Rose was having; and (3) apparently my "as long as Rose is happy, I'm happy" feeling only applied when we were in the same country.

She was having fun without me and it sucked.

I swallowed my jealousy like a bad case of acid reflux.

On the home front, things weren't much better. Some lady at the grocery store had glared at Grub while he was undertaking his usual reconnaissance in the dairy aisle, and then—adding insult to injury—she'd mumbled something about "kids being out of control these days."

Mom, predictably, took it like an enraged she bear.

"The nerve of that woman!" she ranted while doing dishes that night.

"Well, it couldn't hurt for Grub to behave a little more normally, at least in public," I said, drying the plate she handed me.

Mom glared at me as if I'd just denounced oxygen. "Don't tell me you're siding with her intolerant small-town parenting mumbo jumbo."

I recoiled slightly but held my ground. "All I'm saying is maybe she has a point. I mean, the kid's best friend is an elderly Alzheimer's patient. Not to mention the whole white-and-yellow food thing, the World War II obsession, the compulsive mapmaking . . ."

Mom poked her head into the hallway to make sure Grub couldn't hear us. He was still in the living room drawing maps—big surprise. Mom lowered her voice and pointed at me with a sudsy spatula. "There's nothing wrong with that boy, do you hear me? I'll take him back to Chicago before I deal with this kind of claptrap judgment."

I wiped some spatula soap from my cheek, then took a deep breath. "I'm serious, Mom, I'm a little worried about him. Blackjack hasn't been doing so well. Sometimes he doesn't even remember who Grub is. And that army game they play has been walking a fine line between reality and fiction lately."

Mom raised an eyebrow and continued on. "Well, it's still better than what most kids his age are doing, staring at screens and numbing their minds. And besides, you're always with him at Hilltop, right?"

"Well, yeah, but . . ." I paused. That wasn't exactly true, or was it? I guess it depended on whether Mom meant with him *generally* or with him *in the same room*. In either case, I decided now was not a good time to ask. Whenever Mom's parenting skills got questioned, there was hell to pay. Maybe I'd bring it up again after she cooled down.

"In fact, I think what Manny's doing is a wonderful thing. He's expressing his creativity and learning from his elders. All those years Grandma was sick, I was so grateful when people took the time to talk to her, to treat her with compassion. That's what Manny's doing with Mr. Porter. Your brother has a good heart. He's a special—"

"Special snowflake, I get it, Mom." I raised my white flag in surrender, and then used it to dry the spatula. I decided if Mom wasn't going to worry about him, I wouldn't either. I changed the subject. "So what are you making for that catering job at the nursing home? Letty's birthday party."

"I can't even think about that right now, I'm so pissed at that grocery store woman."

"Everyone loves your triple chocolate brownies."

"I don't own a damn confectionery," she snapped.

I threw my hands in the air, conceding defeat. We finished the dishes in silence. Mom mostly grumbled to herself for the next few days, and I kept my distance.

The one small ray of sunshine during an otherwise bleak stretch was the amount of time I spent with Dylan, Axl, and Novie. And that went well for about one whole day until Dylan's girlfriend dumped him.

That evening, Axl and Novie had decided to play some songs for their great-grandmother's birthday party, so we'd been going through Letty's handwritten list in Dylan's basement. After crossing off song after song, we'd narrowed our selections to two: "Life Could Be a Dream" and "These Boots Are Made for Walkin'."

"What time does the party start?" asked Dylan.

"Six o'clock," I replied.

"Right on. Our first official show as a band," said Axl.

"Nursing Home Tour!" said Novie, crossing her sticks over her head, followed by a drumroll and a cymbal crash.

"Gotta start somewhere, right?" said Dylan.

While there was some humor to the circumstance, it truly was our first gig as a band, as well as my first time playing in front of a crowd. We wanted to sound good, regardless of the audience.

"Who's going to be there?" I asked. "Besides the residents, I mean."

"Pretty much our whole family," said Novie. "Mom, grandparents, aunts, uncles, friends. Most of our cousins." Novie paused and wagged her eyebrows at Dylan. "*DeeDee* will be there."

"You know I have a girlfriend," said Dylan from behind his guitar.

"She asked how you've been," Novie replied, still moving her eyebrows.

"No way," said Dylan. His phone dinged in his pocket. "See? Anna's listening from across the country. She just texted. Be right back." Dylan hurried across the basement to attend to his phone.

"Who's DeeDee?" I asked.

"Our second cousin. She met Dylan a couple years ago and totally had the hots for him," said Novie. "Unfortunately, she inherited the Kowalczyk crazy genes. She's tenacious."

"And persistent," added Axl.

"She's tenaciously persistent," said Novie.

"Completely nuts," said Axl, accentuating his point by slapping a string on his bass, which sounded like a spring flying loose.

"Batshit," said Novie, twirling a drumstick in a circular motion next to her head. "So, Zeus, how are things with Rose? Is she back yet?"

"Things are good. She gets back in a couple days. I'm playing a song with her too for this shindig, if we have enough time to learn one." I almost hoped we didn't. The thought of playing music with Rose still flustered me.

"Sweet," said Novie.

Dylan groaned from across the room. We all turned to see him slowly making his way back to the practice space. He looked as if he might barf. "Dr Pepper me. Now."

"Are you okay?" asked Novie.

Axl reached in the fridge, popped open a can, and handed it to Dylan. "What's wrong, dude?"

Dylan collapsed into the couch and took a long swig. He belched. "Anna dumped me." He belched again. "For some other camp counselor in Maine. She said 'he's really nice' and that I'll have to meet him." Dylan mumbled a series of profanities, then took another drink. "Two years down the drain. I knew it was a bad idea for her to go away this summer."

I looked at the twins out of the corner of my eye for a reaction. They were doing the same to each other.

"That sucks, dude," Novie finally said.

"We should have seen it coming," Axl added.

"*I* didn't even see it coming," said Dylan to no one.

"Are you sure you read the text right? What did it say, exactly?" I asked.

Dylan pulled out his phone and started scrolling. "Blah, blah, 'I think we need to spend some time apart,' something about having our whole lives ahead of us, then 'You're a really special person and I hope we can stay friends.'"

"Ouch," said Novie.

"Yeah, she definitely dumped you, man," said Axl.

I nervously picked at a string, then scratched at a spot on the guitar with my thumbnail, suddenly finding it incredibly interesting. Novie popped a bubble of chewing gum. Axl scratched his head.

"She dumped me," Dylan said. *"She dumped me,"* he repeated, emphasizing every word.

"Screw Anna, Nursing Home Tour!" Axl yelled with a fist pump.

Dylan looked at him blankly.

All this girlfriend talk drove my thoughts into their favorite rest stop—Rose. What was she doing right then? My gut twisted at the thought of the entire island of Saint Thomas admiring Rose in a swimsuit. *I'd* never even seen Rose in a swimsuit. What the hell. What if she met someone else, like Anna did? I wasn't sure how well I could handle that news. Not nearly as well as Dylan had, anyway.

The film rolled in my mind.

Action!

Wide aerial shot of a crowd gathered on the beach. Next shot, from the ground. A helicopter approaches from the horizon. Zoom to a close-up of my face. A five o'clock shadow shows the hardships of my travels. I lean out the door and the wind blows my hair. The pilot asks, "Are you ready, Mr. Gunderson?" I lower my Ray-Bans and reply, "I'm always ready." One final check of my straps and I swan dive from the door. As I plummet toward the ocean, I see the heads turn—the heads surrounding the girl in the canvas beach chair. I'd heard tales of her beauty. Just before I hit the water, the bungee catches and my tear-away clothes fall off, revealing my bulging Speedo. The crowd on the beach gasps as the sun reflects off my copper, washboard abs. I ascend from the recoil, reach the apex, then tumble into a ball while simultaneously releasing my harness. Three flips and a jackknife later I return to meet the water with a splashless dive.

New shot, from the beach. I reemerge being pulled ashore by two dolphins, one on either side. The crowd is applauding. Slow-motion shot of me walking out of the water onto the white sand, approaching the camera. Water drips from my body. The crowd parts, and Rose lies before me, glistening in the sun. One man remains. He releases his blue hair from its knot and it spills to his shoulders. He peers menacingly at me through yellow-framed glasses. He looks at Rose, licks his lips, then nods to me. "What are you going to do about it?" he asks. I calmly approach him and remove my Ray-Bans. "Step away, or deal with this." I point to myself with both thumbs. His face turns craven and he bows away, apologizing. The crowd cheers. The girl looks at me. "Mr. Gunderson," she says. "Miss Santos," I say. She extends a hand, which I take. I tuck a lock of her black hair behind her ear, then gently tilt her head back with a lift of her chin. I lean in and—

"Ground Control to Major Zeus, do you copy?" said Axl.

I blinked a couple times and looked around, reacquainting myself with my surroundings. Axl was looking at me. He had asked me something. I should reply. I scanned my brain for context. None. Shit. *Say something neutral and noncommittal*, I thought.

"Oh, well, you know how that goes."

Axl made a face and looked at his sister, then back to me. "I said, are you free to practice tomorrow night?"

"Oh, right. Yeah, sure."

"Cool, we'll pick you up."

Dylan made a groaning sound that startled Agatha awake

from her dog dreams. He appeared to be rereading the text on his phone.

"Maybe we should . . ." I motioned toward the stairs with my head.

"Right," said Novie. She and her brother stood.

Axl slapped Dylan on the shoulder. "We're here for you, bud. You don't need her anyway. Same time tomorrow."

"I'll let DeeDee know you're coming," said Novie as she walked past Dylan, patting him on the head.

Dylan dry heaved.

We practiced every night that week. The songs sounded mediocre at best, with our guiding light suffering from acute heartbreak. But I'd like to think our presence helped with Dylan's overall morale, at least a little bit.

After the ten longest days of my life, Rose returned home on a red-eye flight. I biked to her apartment before my deliveries just to see her.

We met with a long embrace.

"I missed you," Rose said.

"I missed you, too."

I could still smell the ocean in her hair.

TWENTY-SEVEN

AFTER WEEKS OF POSTPONEMENT, MOM FINALLY SCHEDULED OUR annual trip to see Aunt Willow, an art teacher and painter by trade. My aunt's cottage was only a two-hour drive north to Wisconsin on Geneva Lake, but when I found out we were leaving the day after Rose returned from Saint Thomas, it may as well have been the Arctic Circle. I know, I know, what's one or two more days when it's already been ten, right? But when has logic ever trumped the heart?

So, after some pro-level negotiating, I'd gotten Mom to allow Rose to join us under the *strict* guidelines that we'd sleep in opposite corners of the house. *Got it, Mom.*

We met Saturday in front of the café after Mom had closed everything up. The plan was to return Monday morning in time to open. Mary had dropped Rose off with her things, but not before a full debriefing. Mom assured Mary she'd keep an eye on us, and that all would be well, as if we were on our way to the moon, not Wisconsin.

Mom had worked out a deal with Mo the psychic to borrow her SUV in exchange for free lunch the rest of the summer. The Lego had developed a suspicious rattle and would be spending the weekend at the mechanic's infirmary.

"Thanks again, Mo, we really appreciate it," said Mom.

Mo waved it off. "Keep that delicious food coming and you can use it anytime."

"Anything we should know before we leave?" I asked. "Potholes to avoid? Traffic jams? Bad spirits?"

Mo lowered her gaze at me. "I'm a palm reader, not a fortune cookie."

"Duly noted," I replied.

We threw our bags in the back, then took our seats. Mom drove, Grub grabbed shotgun, Rose and I rode bazooka. As soon as Mom started the engine, a psychedelic, guitar-laced jam blasted from the car speakers.

"I should've known Mo was a Deadhead! I love these guys." Mom exclaimed, turning the volume up even louder as we drove away from the café.

Rose and I shared an apprehensive look. While our musical tastes didn't overlap much, clearly neither of us wanted to listen to the Grateful Dead for the next two hours.

Twenty minutes later we were heading north on the

interstate, and the same damn song was playing. Mom drummed on the steering wheel. Grub had fallen asleep. I stared at the ceiling as endless guitar solos swirled around bouncy bass lines. After another ten minutes, I couldn't take it anymore. "Do they ever actually sing? I don't know how much more noodling I can listen to."

"It doesn't need words, Zeus. They're improvising. Listen to what the guitar is saying," Mom replied, weaving her head to the beat.

Rose chimed in. "It's true. A lot of my favorite songs are instrumental."

I jokingly rolled my eyes. "Okay, you two, but we're on a road trip. We need something we can *sing* to. Something with words."

"All right, we'll take turns then," said Mom. "Zeus, you first. Make it a good one."

I plugged my phone into the auxiliary port in the back of the center console and played "London Calling" by the Clash. The opening guitar chords came crashing out with the drums. I played air bass as it joined in. Then I turned to Rose and mouthed the lyrics: *"London calling to the faraway towns, now war is declared and battle come down."* Rose laughed at my obnoxious lip-synching but nodded her head along with the beat. When the song ended, I motioned with both hands palms up. "See? The Clash rocks."

"Good choice," said Rose. "Okay, Coriander, you go next. I'm still thinking."

Mom played Bob Dylan's "Baby, Let Me Follow You Down," singing along loudly and out of key, which was saying a lot as far as Bob Dylan goes. When the song ended, Mom said, "No one writes songs like that anymore. Whatever happened to three chords and a message?"

"I hear what you're saying," said Rose. "But do you two know any songs written in *this* millennium?" Mom and I shared a look in the rearview mirror. Rose shook her head in amusement. "I've got the perfect song to bring you into the twenty-first century. Check it out."

"Somebody That I Used to Know" by Gotye slowly crept out of the speakers like a genie from a lamp. It took a little while to gain momentum, but by the second chorus we'd started a new dance craze, as much as our seat belts would allow. I'd always assumed it was an older song, since in my mind, old music = good, new music = bad. But it turned out that good music *had* been written in the last few years.

For the rest of the ride we continued our rotation. I played the Sex Pistols; Rose played Of Monsters and Men. Mom played Widespread Panic; I played Naked Raygun. The two-hour ride flew by, marked by a few isolated thunderstorms and one quick bathroom break. Grub sat out the musical conversation, but I occasionally caught the top of his army helmet bobbing along.

Our genre swapping soon evolved into a new game: Musical Guilty Pleasures—you know, the one that inevitably ends with Queen's "Bohemian Rhapsody" or "Hey Ya!" by OutKast. As we entered the town of Williams Bay, Wisconsin, Mom rolled down the windows and we all chanted the swelling chorus to "Come On Eileen" by Dexys Midnight Runners.

"Come on! Eileen taloo-rye-aye, come on! Eileen taloo-rye-aye!"

The song faded to an end as we turned onto my aunt's street. The lake came into view for the first time and I took a deep breath, taking it all in. The road led directly to the water-front, where tall oaks guarded the shore like a fortress wall. My aunt's cottage, six houses up from the lake, lay surrounded by lush greenery and flowers, all perfectly in bloom. As we pulled into the driveway, we spotted Aunt Willow on the front porch wearing a sun hat over her long, side-braided hair. She greeted us with warm hugs and crinkly-eyed smiles. After I introduced her to Rose, we headed inside to unpack.

While Mom, Aunt Willow, and Grub got caught up, I gave Rose a quick tour of the cottage. I explained how every single decoration and picture had a story—the wooden oar hanging on the wall had been made in 1873 and subsequently purchased from an antique dealer in Elkhorn; the small rocking chair in the corner was the very one Mom and Aunt Willow's own grandfather had been rocked to sleep in; the blond-haired boy about to eat a minnow in the photograph was, in fact, me at the age of two before my hair color changed.

The fate of the minnow remained uncertain.

After the tour, we headed to the lakeshore to partake in a family tradition: carry-out spaghetti and meatballs. It was the one day of the year Mom ate meat. We sat in Adirondack chairs in a semicircle facing the lake, eating from our aluminum to-go containers. The water shimmered in the early evening sun like blue and white sequins. Across the bay, nearly a mile away, multimillion-dollar mansions jutted from the earth atop emerald-green lawns the size of football fields.

Aunt Willow, who'd seated herself between me and Rose, began one of her intense inquiries—not out of nosiness, but sincere interest.

"Cori tells me you're a *musician*," said my aunt to Rose. The way she said *musician* was the same way someone might say *astronaut*—full of awe.

Rose nodded with a mouthful of spaghetti. "Mm-hmm."

"You know, Sol and I—that's my late husband—we loved going to the Chicago Symphony Orchestra when we lived there. Have you ever been?"

"No, but I'd love to," Rose replied.

"Well, maybe Zeus can take you there with all his hard-earned tip money," said my aunt, patting me on the knee, then turning back to Rose. "You're a pianist, yes?"

Rose nodded again. "I'm working on it."

"She's really good," Grub said. "She's going to piano school next year."

Rose and I exchanged a look.

"Oh, lovely," replied my aunt before we could correct him. "We had a piano growing up, didn't we, Cori? Not that it got used much. We could barely pound out 'Mary Had a Little Lamb' with one finger!"

Aunt Willow continued telling stories about failed music lessons, making everyone laugh, including Rose. I'd known the two of them would get along, and I was happy to see them hit it off. But another part of me counted the seconds until I could have some alone time with Rose, which hadn't happened since her return from Saint Thomas.

"Is this your first time seeing Geneva Lake, Rose?" my aunt asked.

"Yes, it's beautiful!"

"There *is* something magical about it," Aunt Willow agreed. "Tomorrow morning we'll take out the boat first thing and give you a tour. Did you bring your swimsuit?"

"Yep, it's in my bag," Rose replied.

I tried to control my breathing. Picturing her in a swimsuit had taken up most of my brain space for the past week.

My aunt continued. "And how was the drive up? Did you run into any rain?"

"A little," Rose replied. "It was a great ride though. We all took turns playing our favorite music."

"How fun!" said my aunt. She put a finger to her chin. "Let me guess, Zeus played his loud guitar music and Cori played her hippie music." Aunt Willow leaned over and put her hand on Rose's arm. "And you played them some *real* music." I couldn't see my aunt's face, but based on Rose's reaction, she'd just received one of Aunt Willow's classic winks, which made you feel like you were the only person that mattered to her.

Rose shrugged with a grin. "It's all *real* music, I guess, just a matter of taste."

"It's also a road trip," I added. "You need songs with words on road trips."

"Oh, nonsense," my aunt replied. "Some of my best ideas come while driving and listening to the classics."

"I guess I just don't get classical music," I confessed.

"Maybe it's like broccoli," Mom said.

"Gross," said Grub. He'd finished eating his breadsticks and noodles—no meatballs or sauce for him—and had begun setting up miniature plastic army men in various formations on his chair.

"Zeus, when you were two you absolutely despised broccoli," Mom explained. "The sight, the smell—the mere mention of it made you retch."

My face turned red.

"Aww!" said Rose.

Redder.

Mom continued. "So everyone knows broccoli is a good source of dietary fiber. And Zeus used to get so constipated—"

"Mom!" I glared at her. Rose snorted and choked on her spaghetti.

"Oh, don't be embarrassed, everybody poops," Mom said, waving a hand dismissively.

"And your point is?" I asked.

"So I read somewhere that it can take up to fifteen tries to get a kid to eat broccoli before his taste buds acclimate to it. And that's about what it took with you. You eat it now like it's no big deal! My *point* is, maybe it's the same with music."

My aunt directed a meatball-tipped fork at her sister. "I think you're onto something."

Mom continued. "So at first, classical music may taste like broccoli, but after enough tries it may taste like, I don't know..." She held up her food tray. "Spaghetti and meatballs."

Aunt Willow walked over to my mom with a bottle of wine and refilled her glass. "Little sister, you get wiser by the day. Cheers."

Across the lake, a crescent moon rose like a neon-white thumbnail clipping. Eventually, Mom and Aunt Willow took Grub back to the cottage to play Monopoly, but Rose and I stayed by the water a while longer. Though it had gone unspoken, both of us had been waiting for this moment of privacy for what seemed like an eternity. I'd been eyeing the hammock hovering between two trees near the shore.

"I have an idea," I whispered.

"Hammock?"

I smiled back at her. "You read my mind."

As we stood, I noticed the half-full bottle of wine my aunt had left behind. I glanced over my shoulder. Coast was clear. I snagged the bottle.

"What are you doing?" asked Rose in a way that was not so much accusatory as complicit and excited.

"Come on!" I whispered. I took her by the hand and led her between the ancient oaks to the waterfront. We kicked off our shoes and stood on either side of the hammock. After a brief discussion over the best way not to catapult each other into the water, we counted to three and fell into the yarn-like mesh. It folded us into the middle like a couple of netted codfish.

Not such a bad thing.

I pulled the cork out of the bottle with my teeth, which made a loud *THOOP*!

"*Shhh!* I don't want to get caught," whispered Rose.

"Don't worry, they'll never know." I offered her a drink.

Rose smiled, but shook her head. "You first."

I put the bottle to my lips and took a swig. It was much more sour than I expected, but it instantly made my stomach feel warm and tingly. "A very fine vintage," I joked. "Now you."

Rose held the bottle with both hands, took a tiny sip, then

I smiled mysteriously. "Want to hear it right now?"

"Well, yeah! But you didn't bring your guitar," said Rose.

"One minute." I walked outside and grabbed my guitar, which rested right where I'd left it: ten feet away, below the window. Strands of twine still hung from it, which I'd used to strap it to my back for the ride across town. I'd hidden it behind the bushes, just in case my apology backfired, or I chickened out, which both seemed likely scenarios.

I walked inside. "How'd this get here?" I asked, looking as if it had fallen out of the sky.

Rose grinned from ear to ear.

"Let's see," I strummed a chord to make sure it was in tune. It wasn't. It didn't matter. I began to play. And then, because it was just her—just *us*—I decided to sing, too.

"To lead a better life . . . I need my love to be here."

Rose covered a smile with both hands.

As I sang, I could tell my face had flushed red, but I didn't care. A quick glance at Rose was all it took to keep me going. I had almost made it through the entire song. It certainly wasn't great, but I was giving it my best effort.

"I will be there and everywhere . . . here, there, and everywhere." I strummed the last chord and made a ta-da motion with my picking hand.

Rose jumped off the couch, threw her arms around me, and kissed me on the cheek, sandwiching the guitar between us. "I

TWENTY-SIX

SO MUCH HAPPENED OVER THE NEXT FEW WEEKS THE DAYS BLURRED together. Monday after the Art Institute, as if his ears were burning, Rose's dad asked her to join him on a last-minute trip to Saint Thomas in the Virgin Islands. Sounds great, right? Well, yes and no. First of all, it'd be Rose's introduction to her new stepfamily, which didn't thrill her. Second—and possibly more important—it meant a whole week of us apart. In the end, she decided that accepting the invitation was the right thing to do and left a few days later.

We decided we'd talk on the phone every night, and reminded each other it was only seven days. But the night they arrived at the resort, her dad won an extra three nights for attending some time-share presentation. They rescheduled their flights, and seven days became ten days. Then we found out flashed her eyes wide. "It's good!" she whispered, then took another.

We each took a couple more drinks before I put the cork back in the bottle and stuck it between us.

"Thanks for bringing me here," said Rose after a while.

I gazed at Rose, her face painted inky blue from the dim moonlight. She looked like a movie star. I almost blurted out how I felt about her, something I'd wanted to tell her for a while, but lost my courage and laughed through my nose.

"What?" Rose asked.

I shook my head. "Nothing. Just *you*."

Rose moved her legs against mine. Her skin was so smooth. I could taste the wine on her lips.

Around midnight, Rose and I walked back to my aunt's cottage and buried the empty wine bottle at the bottom of her recycling bin. Rose had been given the downstairs guest room, while I'd be claiming an air mattress in the attic. We kissed good night in the kitchen.

Twice.

Three times.

Eventually, Rose went to her room and I walked up the creaky attic stairs.

TWENTY-EIGHT

I WOKE TO THE SOUND OF A BIRD DIRECTLY OUTSIDE THE ATTIC WINdow. Its relentless alarm came in question form: *Po-tee-weet?*
Po-tee-weet? I decided the human translation was either "Are you up?" or "Where all the ladies at?"

I opened one blurry eye to check my phone. 10:13.

Shit!

I overslept.

I rolled off my half-deflated air mattress—a maneuver about as graceful as slipping on ice—and threw on trunks and a fresh shirt. Down the stairs I stumbled, rubbing sleep from my eyes. I burst through the door at the bottom expecting to see everyone at the breakfast table, but it sat empty.

Not empty—there was a note.

Zeus,

Hope you slept well. We're down on the pier. Feel free to heat up breakfast leftovers in the microwave.

—A. W.

After inhaling a cold vegetarian breakfast burrito, I headed for the water.

The pier had already begun to fill with people. I zigged around beach chairs and zagged under umbrellas. At the end of the pier, Rose sat on a wooden bench with my family, wearing a bright yellow bikini that showed all the right things.

"Hey there, sleepyhead. I like the new look." She passed a hand over my hair as I sat next to her. "It goes well with the crease marks on your face." She traced a line along my cheek where my face had been mashed into the pillow.

"Very funny," I said, smoothing my hair down.

"Who's ready for a boat ride?" asked my aunt, dangling the keys.

Soon, Aunt Willow's twenty-one-foot maroon Wellcraft Sportsman, which I'd nicknamed the SS *Ron Burgundy*, was backing out from its lift. Rose and I sat up front, Aunt Willow drove, Mom rode shotgun, and Grub sat crouched in the back with his Nerf gun aimed at the shore.

As we made our way out of the bay and into the lake proper, we veered left, hugging the shoreline. Aunt Willow gave us a guided tour, pointing out various lakefront homes: the Wrigley Estate; the Playboy Club Hotel, Hugh Hefner's original Playboy Mansion; the Driehaus Estate, famous for its million-dollar party every year with changing themes. I imagined their owners frolicking in diamonds and blowing their noses with wads of hundred-dollar bills. And then I pictured our Buffalo Falls apartment, and me riding Mom's old Schwinn across the bridge delivering salads. The injustice I felt at that moment registered somewhere shy of jealous and a hair past envious, hovering around bitter. But the feeling soon passed when Rose crossed her bare feet over mine. I looked at her in that bikini, wishing I'd worn sunglasses. The curves, the belly button, the bouncing, the—

"See that one?" My aunt pointed to another mansion. "The woman who lives there owns an art gallery where I sell some of my paintings. She's having her big summer soirée tonight."

I looked at the labyrinthine landscaping that cut its way uphill, where a four-story brick house shadowed a sprawling lawn. A large white tent had been set up in the yard, and uniformed workers buzzed around it like bees. It was one of the fanciest properties we'd seen yet.

"How cool would it be to go to *that* party?" said Rose.

My aunt laughed. "We can go if you like. All I have to do is let Sylvia know. She invited me, but I didn't want to cancel plans with you guys."

Rose looked at me eagerly. "Want to go?"

"Are you sure you want to hang around a bunch of old artsy people?" I asked.

"Watch it, buster!" said my aunt with a wink. "We're not all ancient. Besides, Sylvia mentioned her grandson and his friends would be there. They're about your age, I think."

I looked back at Rose, who had plastered a cheesy smile on her face and held her hands folded under her chin—a face you couldn't say no to.

"All right, count us in," I said.

Rose squealed.

"Don't keep them out too late, sis, we have to be up early," Mom said. "I'll stay back and read my book. Manny, maybe you can work in Aunt Willow's studio and draw one of your super-sized maps on a canvas?"

"Roger that!" he shouted from underneath the beach towel fortress he'd constructed in the back of the boat.

"Party starts at eight, so we should leave by seven," said my aunt. "We'll take the boat over. How about we head back and grab some lunch, then you guys can have the rest of the after-noon to yourselves before we go?"

"Great!" said Rose. She grinned and spun to face me, prop-ping her legs up on my lap.

"Great," I agreed, trying not to appear as crazy-happy as I felt.

* * *

That evening, after a brief panic over dress-code concerns, Aunt Willow drove us across the lake to the party. The sun hadn't set yet, but the eastern sky had begun to grow a deep violet. Yellow sparkles peppered the lakefront as homes turned on their lights for the night.

Once there, a group of men in polo shirts greeted us at the pier, offering free valet docking service. While some of the vintage wooden boats and small yachts had been granted mechanical lift access, smaller boats, such as the SS *Ron Burgundy*, were moored to buoys a small distance from the pier.

We walked up a winding pathway, lit on either side by small, solar-powered lights. Ivy-covered stones tiered the hill into three levels. Near the top, we began to hear the buzz of conversation. As we cleared the summit, dozens of people came into view, talking, eating, and drinking, while servers with silver trays circulated between them. The imposing house behind everyone looked more like a resort than a home—the windows alone were twenty feet tall.

A white-haired woman came waltzing over to us as we took it all in. "Willow! So glad you could make it, darling. And this is your niece and nephew?"

"This is my nephew, Zeus, and this is his—" My aunt looked to me for confirmation.

"Girlfriend. Rose," I confirmed, taking Rose's hand.

"*Zeus and Rose*, now isn't that marvelous? It reminds me of the theater, I don't know why, ah-ha-ha-ha! I'm Sylvia, it's a pleasure." She shook our hands. I got the impression she loved playing hostess. "Zeus, your aunt is an incredible artist, you do know this, yes?"

"I do," I replied.

"The *best*. Come, follow me. The other young people are just over here."

Sylvia led us across the lawn to the veranda, where her grandson and his friends sat in a circle staring at their phones. "Jake, darling, this is Willow's nephew, Zeus, and his friend, Rose. They're here visiting from Illinois."

"What's up," said Jake, never looking away from his phone.

"Won't you introduce your friends?" asked Sylvia.

Jake continued looking at his phone, but pointed to the others. "J. B., John, Dave, Todd, Mikey, and Domingo."

"What's up," they all muttered, more or less in unison.

"Willow, come with me," said Sylvia. "Let's get you a glass of champagne."

"Have fun," said my aunt as Sylvia whisked her away.

I looked at Rose and offered my arm. "Shall we mingle?" We approached the group, whose names I'd already forgotten except for Jake. They all wore various colors of deck shorts and boat shoes and all of their faces remained buried in their phones. I wondered if they were communicating with one another, or simply existing in the same physical space separately.

"Where're you from in Illinois?" asked the one in pink shorts.

"Buffalo Falls," I said.

"Never heard of it," replied Pink Shorts.

"Me neither," said Yellow Shorts.

"I have." Blue Shorts momentarily put his phone down to inspect us for the first time. "My parents used to take me to that state park lodge when I was little."

"Metea State Park," I said.

"Yeah. It was lame," said Blue Shorts. Then he went back to his phone. None of them offered us a seat, so we continued to stand.

"So, what do you *do* in Buffalo Falls?" asked Jake, big emphasis on the second *do*. From the way he held his phone, I could tell he was positioning for the perfect selfie.

"Uh, it's small, so . . ." I thought about what we'd done that summer—polka dancing, palm reading, salad deliveries, geriatric puzzle assembly—not acceptable answers. "We usually just hang out."

Rose took over. "Do all of you guys live around here?"

"My parents have a place across the lake," said Pink Shorts, "but we all live in Chicago."

"Oh really? Zeus is from Chicago originally," said Rose.

That made Jake look up from his phone. "Yeah? Where at?"

"South Side, by Midway," I replied.

"Oh," he said, making me feel like I'd answered wrong.

"Where in Chicago are you guys from?" I asked.

"Highland Park," said Orange Shorts, who hadn't spoken until now. I was about to inform him that Highland Park, an affluent suburb home to the likes of Michael Jordan and other multimillionaires, was decidedly *not* in Chicago, but I bit my tongue.

"Right on," I said.

We stood in silence for a moment. Then Rose spoke again. "You guys must love it up here. It's beautiful. This house is amazing."

"Yeah," said Jake.

"It's decent," said Yellow Shorts.

It was beyond clear that Jake and the colorful-shorts crew had zero interest in us.

Rose whispered in my ear, "Maybe we should go mingle with *ourselves*, if you know what I mean."

"Do I ever," I whispered back. "Let's go."

TWENTY-NINE

ROSE AND I WANDERED AROUND THE PROPERTY UNTIL WE FOUND A wooden bench swing facing the lake. We sat, my arm around Rose while she rested her head on my shoulder—a move we'd mastered at that point. Her hair smelled like lilacs with a hint of lake water. The sun had just begun to sink beyond the horizon, painting the clouds in deck-shorts pink.

"Seriously, how can their phones be more interesting than this place?" asked Rose.

I shook my head. "I guess when you've grown up with all this, you take it for granted."

Rose let out a soft sigh and stroked the hair on my arm. We watched the last wink of sunlight slip out of view. Lightning flickered across the lake. We waited for the thunder, but it was still too far away.

"Maybe it's like what we talked about before, about heaven," said Rose.

"Like, if everything's great all the time, how can you tell?"

"Exactly. I bet those guys grew up with everything they ever wanted. Coming here is probably just another day. An inconvenience, even."

Two ducks flew across our view.

"I wonder what their heaven is?" I asked.

Rose chortled, then in a ditzy valley-girl accent said, "Probably, like, the perfect selfie."

I laughed, then mimicked a bro voice. "Dude, did you notice my deck shorts match my phone case?"

"Uh, yeah! Hello? I just tweeted about it."

We both laughed and I pulled her closer.

Thunder rumbled across the water. God either disapproved of our heaven talk or had just bowled a perfect strike. The surface of the water seemed to blur where the rain made contact. Another flash of lightning, this time with only a three-second delay before the *CRACK!* and rumble.

"Holy shitballs," I said. "We're going to get drenched!"

The wind picked up as we turned for the house. The temperature felt like it had dropped fifteen degrees. Ahead, the partygoers scrambled to rush inside. The first fat, cold drops hit our heads, followed by a *whoosh* as the downpour swept up the hill after us. Lightning cracked again, this time with no delay between flash and sound.

"Hurry!" yelled Rose.

We made it inside just before getting soaked. Everyone crowded into a marble-floored foyer. The catering staff scurried around with serving trays and carts, getting everything inside, out of the storm.

Sylvia climbed a few steps up the central staircase and addressed the party. "Everyone! Everyone! We won't let a little storm get in the way of a good time. If you'd all follow the hall to the right, we'll resume in the great room. Eat! Drink! Be merry!"

Rose and I followed the herd into the great room, which was aptly named. We sat in a corner on two mahogany-colored leather chairs. The party guests filed in, and the murmur of conversation grew to a low buzz. I noticed a grand piano in the opposite corner.

I nudged Rose, pointing to it with my chin.

She looked, squinted, then her eyes went wide. "Is that a *Steinway*?"

"No, it's a *piano*," I said.

Rose swatted my leg. "Let's go look!"

We shuffled through the crowd to the piano. Embossed above the keys was *Steinway & Sons*. "You were right," I said.

Rose ran her fingers along the smooth, polished wood.

"God, this probably cost sixty thousand dollars."

"Eighty," said Jake, who had walked up behind us with a couple of his friends.

"That's insane," I said, shaking my head.

Jake shrugged. "We have one at home. It never gets used though."

Just then, Sylvia showed up with my aunt. "Zeus, I'm told we have quite the pianist in our presence." She smiled at Rose.

"Yeah, play them a little Tom Jones," I said, poking her in the arm.

"I don't think this is a Tom Jones crowd," she said under her breath.

"Just one song!" Sylvia urged. "There's sheet music inside the bench."

Rose thought for a moment. "That's okay, I don't need it. There's one I've been working on."

"Marvelous!" said Sylvia, splashing around her champagne. "And what's the song?"

"*Raindrop Prelude* by Frédéric Chopin," said Rose. She sat at the bench, uncovered the keys, and began.

The first notes hung in the air, soft. Then her right hand drummed two repetitive notes while her left hand climbed around a dark minor melody. It got louder. It got darker. I glanced over my shoulder to see interested heads turn; a few walked toward the piano. Halfway through the song, Jake and the deck-shorts crew had turned their phones away from themselves and toward Rose, filming. I looked back at Rose. Rain trickled down the windowpane behind her as the music dripped from her fingertips. She hit some of the chords so hard I felt them in my chest. A crowd had now formed near the piano. All were silent.

Aunt Willow whispered in my ear, "What the hell is that girl doing in Buffalo Falls?"

It was then that I knew. More completely than I'd ever known anything before. My aunt was right; Rose didn't belong in Buffalo Falls. All this time, I'd known she was good, but I truly had no idea just *how* good she was. She'd made an entire room of people—hell, an entire wing of a mansion—go silent. She was *that* good. She was brilliant.

The last chord resonated throughout the room. For a moment, the only sound was the rain on the window. And then the room erupted into applause. Rose turned her head and blinked as if just remembering where she was.

Jake and his crew moved in with a barrage of compliments and questions.

"Dude, that was incredible!" said Jake.

"That was amazing!" said Pink Shorts.

"How did you do that without music?" asked Yellow Shorts.

"She's only been playing for three years," I said. *Let them chew on that little piece of trivia,* I thought.

"Three years? I've been playing since I was *three years old* and can't play like that!" said Yellow Shorts.

"How are you not famous?" asked Jake.

"I'm totally putting that on YouTube," said Blue Shorts.

Rose was a good sport and did a short request set for Jake & Company, who by now were completely enamored. I sat back in proud admiration. After a while, Sylvia approached Rose and whispered something in her ear. Moments later, Rose began Dean Martin's "That's Amore" as Sylvia—this time literally—waltzed through the room. Everyone else soon joined in, except for Jake & Co., who filmed themselves with Rose, urgently posting to their social media accounts.

When Rose finished the song, she looked around the room to find me, then flashed that perfect smile.

That's amore, I thought to myself.

The next morning, my wake-up call came in the form of Mom yelling "Rise and shine!" at four thirty.

I groaned, remembering we had to make it back to Buffalo Falls in time to open the café. Getting up that early should have been illegal.

Rose and I watched the sunrise from the dock while drinking coffee. A blanket of fog drifted toward shore, running for its life from the sun's searching rays. The only other person on the lake was a fisherman who motored by. He waved. We waved back.

"Last night was fun," I said, my voice extra deep from lack of sleep.

"It was." Rose paused to yawn. "But you know what? I wouldn't even know what to do with a house that big. I think your aunt's cottage is just right."

"Maybe it's *who's* in the house that matters, not the *size*."

Rose sipped her drink, then kissed me. "Exactly." Her lips were extra warm from the coffee.

THIRTY

THE FOLLOWING SUNDAY I WHEELED FIVE HEAPING TRAYS OF TRIPLE chocolate brownies into Hilltop, careful not to get any crumbs on my clothes. Letty had insisted everyone dress up for the occasion, so I'd spent the morning at Goodwill with Dylan, Axl, and Novie searching for outfits. Axl chose a black derby hat, Novie bought a black cotton dress and four-inch platform heels, and Dylan found a dark denim button-down shirt he somehow made look cool. I'd picked out a shiny black pair of shoes, wore my best jeans, and a shirt-tie-vest combo with the sleeves rolled up.

I have to admit—we looked pretty damn spiffy.

I'd asked Rose to join us shopping, but she already had something, and said it was a surprise.

Inside Hilltop, the volunteers had outdone themselves with the decorations. Candy was in charge, telling everyone what went where. Letty wore a cone-shaped party hat and followed Candy around, making sure things were to her liking. A dance floor had been cleared in the common room in front of the piano and band equipment, and a long table lined an outer wall, where all the food was to go. Though most of the guests hadn't arrived yet, a buzz of excitement filled the air.

Once through the doors, Grub disappeared down a hallway toward Blackjack's room, yelling something about the final mission. Unfortunately, Blackjack wouldn't be attending the party. His condition hadn't improved, and his nurses had advised he stay in bed.

As Grub scampered away, Mom grumbled something about "expressing himself" and "special snowflake," still heated about the grocery-store lady. I had to hand it to her though—she'd really outdone herself with the menu. She'd whipped up a variety of hors d'oeuvres and desserts, and even some options for those with more restricted diets.

As I wheeled the trays into the room, Rose popped out from around a corner, nearly making me spill the tower of brownies. She wore a red dress with black polka dots, which looked incredible on her. It's funny how just a couple months ago I'd have stammered and stuttered, forcing myself to keep eye contact with her. But today, I drank her in and it felt right.

"You look amazing, Rose," I said.

"Aw, thanks," she said, doing a half spin and exposing a bit of thigh. "And look at you, stud muffin! You clean up nicely," she said, followed by a throat purr.

"Yeah, I think I found a new look," I said, brushing fake dust from my shoulders and pretending to slick my hair back.

"So, are you ready for our big musical debut?"

I wasn't. We'd only rehearsed our duet once, so I'd written down the lyrics and chords on a piece of paper, which I'd stuffed in my back pocket.

"Absolutely," I replied.

"You'll do great," she said, giving me a quick peck on the cheek.

And that's all it took. It *would* be great.

By six fifteen, Hilltop Nursing Home had become a cacophony of conversation, laughter, and music. Letty's guests piled in by the dozens, ranging in mobility from stroller to wheelchair. Having found the triple chocolate brownies, even Missy Stouffer seemed to enjoy herself, though she kept one eye out for misbehavior at all times.

After Letty opened her gifts, which included a life-sized cutout of Tom Jones, she and the Bettys stepped to the stage to perform "Stop! In the Name of Love" by Diana Ross and the Supremes, complete with choreography. Letty, in a gold lamé party pantsuit, was the belle of the ball, her hips swinging and bracelets jangling.

I sat with Dylan, Novie, and Axl, eating, talking, and watching. Dylan nervously scanned the crowd to keep an eye out for crazy cousin DeeDee, though she never did make an appearance. Dylan had been doing a lot better and seemed to be getting over his breakup with Anna. In fact, the number of times he'd checked his phone that morning at Goodwill made us wonder if there might be someone new.

We were all laughing and drilling him for information when Rose stepped up to the microphone. "Mr. Gunderson to the stage, please, Mr. Gunderson to the stage. If I could get everyone's attention, we have a very special song for a very special lady: Letty Kowalczyk!"

Letty strutted to the dance floor with her hands in the air as the crowd cheered and applauded. Someone popped a party streamer at her, resulting in hair full of confetti. She didn't seem to mind.

"Wish me luck," I said to my friends.

"Good luck," said Novie.

"Break a leg," said Axl.

"You got this, man," said Dylan. "Let the music play *you*, don't worry about mistakes."

"Thanks, guys," I said.

I sat by Rose with my guitar and uncrumpled the paper with the lyrics and chords. Rose gave me a wink of encouragement, counted us in, and we began "The Way You Look Tonight" by Frank Sinatra. We shared singing duties, but Rose carried the song musically. Letty danced by herself at first, until one by one family members came out for a turn. Axl, Novie, and their mom, Crash, all had a spin with her, as did other relatives. George Larsen even stepped in for a couple steps before Lucille dragged him away by the arm. Letty looked to be having the time of her life, wiping an occasional tear from her eye.

And while the song was for Letty, Rose and I shared enough private glances to know that it was for us, too.

The party ended with Dylan, Axl, and Novie joining us onstage to perform our two songs, closing the night out with "These Boots Are Made for Walkin'." The dance floor became a melting pot of wheelchairs, walkers, and youth, all inter-mixing and trading partners. Toward the end, a circle formed around Letty, where she executed the Robot, the Sprinkler, and a Michael Jackson kick-spin.

Upon the final cymbal crash, the crowd cheered and Letty took a bow.

Axl leaned over to me, offering a fist bump. "Great job, man!"

"For real. Solid playing," said Novie.

"You, too!" I said.

"Seriously, guys, we sounded tight!" said Dylan. We high-fived and exchanged hugs, Rose included. We'd just completed our first gig, and it felt great.

Meanwhile, Letty had stepped onto the stage and grabbed a microphone. "Ladies and gentleman of Hilltop, friends old and new, and my wonderful family—thank you so much. You know how to throw a great fucking party!"

Missy Stouffer sprung to the stage and snatched the microphone from Letty's hand. "Thank you for coming, everyone, visiting hours are now over. All residents please return to your rooms. Candy, volunteers, please attend to the mess. Thank you."

Letty tapped Missy on the shoulder. "Excuse me, Ms. Stouffer, but my *personal volunteer* will be escorting me to my room."

Missy made a face at me that may have been a smile. "Of course." And then she marched off to her office.

Letty stuck out her elbow for me to grab.

I turned to Rose. "Be right back."

Rose wagged a finger at us. "You two behave now."

Letty winked. "No promises."

I took Letty by the elbow and walked her to her room.

Once inside, she let out a long sigh and sat on the edge of her bed. She kicked off her shoes and rolled her feet around to stretch her ankles. "Pour me some water, kiddo."

As I grabbed the water pitcher, I noticed a framed black-and-white photograph of a young man in military uniform on the nightstand.

"Is that your husband?" I asked.

"That's my Dickey. Just before he got shipped off to France."

He didn't look much older than me.

"Did he . . . make it back?"

"Of course he did. How do you think I pumped out all those kids back there? They weren't sending my Dickey home in a box, oh no sirree. The night he returned . . . well, I won't bore you with the details." She cackled softly to herself, then took the photograph from my hands.

As she gazed upon it, I tried picturing a young Letty and Dickey, their whole lives ahead of them.

She continued. "We didn't have a pot to piss in, but the day he left, he gave me his senior class ring and a promise—a promise to replace it with a real one when he came back. I wore that class ring on my finger for sixteen months. Never took it off until the day he returned. He kept his promise and a month later we were married, then after a year, along came the first of five children. We were married twenty-three years, until his lungs gave out, and I haven't been with another man since. I still have that ring, right there in the top drawer. It's got little red jewels around the edge and says *Class of '42*."

I opened the nightstand drawer, but only saw some stationery, a half dozen pens, and a few loose photographs.

"I don't see it," I said.

Letty kicked her feet up on the bed and lay her head on the pillow. "I'm sure it's there somewhere." She yawned. "Too much dancing."

"Here's your water," I said, handing her the glass.

She sat up and took a long drink. "Thanks. Now go on. You're too young to be hanging out with this old bag of bones. There's a beautiful girl waiting out there for you. Take her somewhere special tonight."

"We're going to the Route 34 Drive-In to see a movie. Axl is letting me borrow his pickup so we can lie down in the back."

Letty nodded, then thought for a moment. "I have a better idea."

"What's that?"

"Take her out to Old Dump Road, all the way until the clearing. It's far from the city lights, the darkest place for miles. You can see the whole Milky Way on a clear night. Is it clear tonight?"

"I think so."

"Good. Go out there, watch the stars. No one will be around. Make some memories; they're better than movies."

Her eyelids started to drift shut. I turned out her lamp, dimming the room to the soft glow of a plug-in nightlight. Letty burrowed under the covers, pantsuit and all, and I tucked her in.

"Happy birthday, Letty. See you tomorrow," I said.

Before I walked away, she grabbed my hand and looked me in the eye. "If there's one thing I've learned in ninety years—remember the good stuff, kiddo. Nothing else matters."

"I'll remember, Letty."

I quietly shut the door.

* * *

Rose and I bounced on the bench seat of Axl's truck like two bobblehead dolls. Old Dump Road lived up to the "old" part, but Old *Pothole* Road would have more accurately described its current state.

Earlier, we'd helped drop off serving trays and catering gear at the café. Every last morsel of food had been consumed at the party, and everyone had raved about it, especially the brownies. Crash took a handful of my mom's business cards and promised to pass them out at the Beauty Saloon. Mom was in such great spirits after that, she'd told us to leave everything in the kitchen, that she'd clean and put it all away herself.

The tall pines on either side of Old Dump Road rose like cliff walls, allowing very little moonlight through. The truck's headlights illuminated thirty feet before us, but night swallowed everything else. After what felt like miles, the pines ended, opening into a field of tall prairie grass covered in dew, glistening in the moonlight. It looked like a painting.

"This must be it," I said.

"It's pretty," said Rose.

I didn't know why my heart was beating so fast. I did a U-turn so the truck bed faced the field, then turned off the engine and the headlights.

"Take a look?"

"Okay," she said. I think she was smiling, but I couldn't see her face in the dark of the truck.

We stepped out and craned our heads back to take in the cloudless sky.

"Letty was right," I said. "That must be the Milky Way, right there." I pointed to a dense band of stars that cut across the sky like a blurry scar.

"There's Orion," said Rose.

"Where?"

"There. You can see the three stars that make up his belt. There's his arms and legs. He's shooting an arrow."

"I still don't see it."

Rose moved behind me. She pointed over my shoulder, resting her arm there. Her warm skin brushed my neck and sent a ripple of goose bumps down my back.

"There," she whispered. Her face was next to mine, and I could smell the sweetness of her breath.

"Got it," I said, although I didn't.

It didn't matter.

We stood like that for a while until she suggested we spread the blankets in the truck bed. I grabbed them from behind the seats and whipped them in the air, then smoothed them out. I lay on my back and wove my fingers behind my head. Rose curled up next to me and rested her head upon my chest. My heart pounded so hard it must have sounded like a kick drum.

"Are you nervous?" she asked.

"A little," I replied. "Are you?"

"A little."

I lay my hand on her side and felt it rise with her breathing, which quickened, as did mine—not out of fear, but the way it might at the top of a roller coaster before the big drop. Her hand found mine and our fingers interlaced. With my free hand I pulled the blanket around us and with the other, her into me.

We both laughed and we both breathed and we both lived. Nothing else mattered except us, right then.

THIRTY-ONE

THE FOLLOWING DAY, I SPENT MY VOLUNTEER HOUR CLEANING UP THE remains of Letty's party. According to one of the Bettys, Letty was napping, still exhausted from her big night. As I stood atop a ladder pulling streamers from the ceiling, I replayed the whole evening in my head over and over, like a movie. From the band playing our first gig to my night under the stars with Rose, everything had been perfect.

Okay, more like imperfectly perfect. Or perfectly imperfect. No need to get bogged down in the details.

Rose and I had shared a look when I'd arrived, but it felt different than previous glances. By then I'd spent countless hours with Rose, but when I walked into Hilltop that afternoon, it felt like nothing needed to be said. We both knew what we both knew, and the private look we exchanged summed it all up.

Grub helped me clean, holding an open garbage bag below my ladder. We'd just finished with the last of the streamers when Mary wheeled out Blackjack, his wispy hair still sleep-matted to his head.

Mary parked her charge, then squatted down in front of Grub. "Hey there, soldier. Blackjack keeps repeating something about a mission, but I'm not sure what he means. I was wondering if you could help me out?"

"Sure." Grub faced the wheelchair and stood at attention. "At your service, sir!"

A scowl twisted Blackjack's face. "Who the hell are you?" he rasped.

Grub's eyes went wide. He looked up at Mary, then at me. He looked back to Blackjack.

"Blackjack, do you remember your friend, Private Grub?" Mary asked, enunciating very clearly.

"It's me," said Grub, taking a careful step toward the wheelchair.

Blackjack stared at him vacantly, then, almost in a whisper, said, "My medals."

Grub paused and looked at us nervously. "Your medals?" he whispered back.

"My medals. They're gone!" Blackjack shouted, lurching forward. Grub leaned back and glanced at me for reassurance, though I wasn't sure what to say. Blackjack continued, his voice dry and scratchy. "Which one of you took them?" He eyed each of us with a ferocity that made my stomach turn.

Mary took over, grabbing Blackjack's hand. "I'm sure your medals are right where they always are."

"Get your hands off me. Someone took them. Which one of you?" A few heads turned in our direction. Blackjack pushed himself up on his wheelchair, trying to stand, but Mary held him down by the shoulders. "Get your hands off me!" he shouted again.

Grub backpedaled and hid behind me.

Mary tried to pacify the old man, but he had worked himself into a rage, red-faced and trembling. A few other nurses rushed over to assist.

Grub grabbed my arm. "Let's go," he said, tugging.

I tried to think of how to explain this to him. I squatted down. "I think Blackjack is having one of those bad days we talked about."

"Who took them?" Blackjack's voice had become distorted, almost as if he were choking. "*Sino ang kumuha nang mga ito?*"

Mary calmly spoke to him in Tagalog while the other nurses helped hold him down. His strength, even now, was impressive.

Grub looked as if he wanted to say something, his brown eyes darting back and forth. I noticed the piano music had stopped, and glanced at Rose, who watched the commotion. She looked worried.

Missy Stouffer briskly entered the room, taking full inventory of the situation within seconds.

"Get your hands off me! Who took them?" Blackjack fought at the nurses.

"Who took what?" Missy asked Mary.

"He's confused. I'll take him back to his room, Ms. Stouffer. He just needs to rest."

Missy flashed me and Grub a suspicious glare.

"Who took my medals?" Blackjack repeated, still struggling.

Missy looked from Blackjack to Mary. "It may very well be confusion; nonetheless, it's my job to take any accusation of stolen property seriously, regardless of the mental state of the person reporting it."

"I've been with him since he woke this morning," Mary replied. "He hasn't left my sight. I'm certain the medals are back in his room. They couldn't possibly be missing."

"Let's be sure then. It'll only take a few minutes to double-check his room." Missy raised her eyebrows at Mary, then nodded toward the hall.

"Of course, Ms. Stouffer," said Mary, who left Blackjack with the other nurses and headed to his room.

Grub still stood by my side, clinging to my shorts. The entire room had focused their attention on us by now. My palms sweated in my pockets. Blackjack had stopped shouting and struggling, but breathed heavily in his wheelchair. The remaining two nurses crouched beside him, muttering soft assurances that he was going to be okay.

Lucille Larsen appeared beside me. "What's the ruckus?"

I leaned in close to her ear. "Blackjack thinks his medals are missing."

"Missing medals? So what's the fuss? I haven't been able to find my wedding ring for weeks and no one seems to care."

Hearing this, Missy turned and scanned her up and down, as if downloading information. "Your wedding ring is missing, Mrs. Larsen?"

Lucille held out her left hand to show Missy Stouffer: no ring.

"I see," said Missy.

A voice called out from behind us, something about rare coins missing.

Another man shouted, "I've been looking for my gold watch for days!"

Grub tugged at my arm again. "I want to go home," he said.

"Now's not a great time. We'll leave in a little bit," I told him.

Mary returned, her shoulders hunched up and palms facing upward. "He's right, I can't find them. I have no idea—"

Before she could finish, Missy pointed to me and the two nurses. "You, you, and you. Check the memory care unit for Mr.

Porter's medals." Then she pointed at Candy. "You talk to the other residents, see if there are more reports of missing property." She pointed at Mary. "You get him calmed down," she said, nodding to Blackjack, who had, for the most part, calmed down. Grub noticed this as well and left my side to join his friend.

Missy and I, along with the two nurses, walked down the long hall of the memory care unit. She ordered them to perform a full sweep of the rooms and took me to the staff lounge. "I can't imagine any of our employees would steal from the residents, but I'd be remiss not to cover all possibilities. Check the cabinets, the lockers, everywhere."

In all the time I'd volunteered at Hilltop, I'd never seen Missy appear anything other than calm and cool. But now she looked rattled and as uncomfortable as I felt to be rooting through other people's belongings.

"Of course," I said, then gulped. My tongue felt like sandpaper on my throat. I wasn't sure why I had been picked to help with the search, but I obliged.

Missy started at one end of the room and I at the other. I opened the cabinets. Nothing out of the ordinary. The closet had everything one might expect. I even checked the refrigerator. Nothing. Finally, I moved on to the employee lockers. Part of me felt invasive; the other part knew I was only following orders.

First locker—empty.

Second locker—a pair of shoes and an umbrella.

Third locker—winner winner, chicken dinner. On the bottom of the locker, underneath a balled-up sweater, lay a pile of old war medals attached to striped ribbons.

"Found 'em," I said to Missy.

She marched across the room and took the medals from the locker. Then she looked the locker up and down. "I see," she said. She turned and walked out the door with haste.

As I shut the locker door, my stomach sank as I recognized Rose's purse.

I ran back to the common room on Missy's heels.

"Mr. Gunderson just found these in your locker," said Missy, holding the medals out to Mary.

I looked at Rose, who furrowed her brow at me in confusion. I opened my eyes wide and shrugged my shoulders.

Mary looked shocked. She actually smiled and shook her head. "That's crazy. How'd they get there?"

"That's a good question, and one I'd like the answer to," said Missy.

Mary searched for words. "Ms. Stouffer, you don't actually think . . . You can't believe *I* took them?"

Missy knelt in front of Blackjack and held up the medals. "Mr. Porter, do you recognize these? Is this your missing property?"

Blackjack slowly lifted his head and spotted the medals in

Missy's hands. His face turned maroon and his chest started heaving again. "Who took them?" he rasped. *"Ibalik nila yan!"*

Missy looked back to Mary.

"Ms. Stouffer, I—I don't know what to say." Mary let out an exasperated breath and dropped her hands to her side. "This is crazy. I don't know how this could have happened."

"Either Mr. Porter is out roaming the halls unattended or someone took them from his room and put them in your locker. In any case, this is a serious breach of responsibility."

"My mom loves Blackjack!" Rose stepped in. "What would she want with his medals? She'd never take them!"

Missy turned to address Rose, but just then, Candy walked up. "Excuse me, Ms. Stouffer, but I've just begun speaking to the residents and have already gotten five more complaints of missing property."

"All from the memory care unit?" asked Missy.

Candy shook her head. "Everywhere."

Missy rubbed the stress from her temples while everyone awaited a response. Blackjack breathed heavily, which sounded more like a rattling wheeze. Mary and Rose exchanged glances. They looked scared. A bead of sweat ran down my back.

Missy spoke, still working at her temples. "This facility is on lockdown until I figure out what's going on. Every square inch will be searched. I'll be speaking with all staff members. If that yields nothing, then I'll call the police and report the thefts." Missy lifted her head, half glaring, half pleading with us to understand. "I will not tolerate this lack of supervision and security under my watch."

Mary blinked and looked at the floor.

I felt about two feet tall.

Blackjack trembled with agitation once again. "Give those back to me! Who took them? Who—" He cut himself off with a heaving cough that turned everyone's head. He gasped for air, then coughed again. Mary, the nurses, and Missy all rushed to his side. He trembled with each breath. Blackjack hacked, then retched on himself.

Missy turned to Mary. "Attend to Mr. Porter. Get him back to his room, cleaned up, and see to any other attention he requires. I'd like to speak to you later. Alone."

"Of course, Ms. Stouffer," said Mary. Rose stood next to her mom, watching. The color had left her face, and she looked as if she might cry.

Amid the chaos, I'd forgotten about Grub. I scanned the room, but he was nowhere to be seen.

"Has anyone seen my brother?" I asked loudly, but everyone was still distracted by Blackjack's meltdown.

I rushed to Rose. "Rose, my brother? Have you seen him?"

She looked at me, wide-eyed, as if she'd just noticed I was there.

"I think I saw him running toward the front door," said one of the Bettys.

Shit.

"Thanks," I said. Then to Rose, "I'll be back later, okay?"

She nodded.

I blew through the front doors, rushed to the sidewalk, and scanned right, then left.

There!

Two blocks down the street, a small, green army helmet bobbed behind a hedgerow, running west.

I hopped on my bike and raced after him, leaving the nursing home in my wake. I caught up to him just as he ran into Dylan's yard.

"Grub, stop! Everything is okay! Blackjack's going to be fine!" I shouted, unsure if those things were true or not.

Grub disappeared behind the house. I let the bike fall to the ground, then followed him into the backyard. I rounded the corner of Dylan's garage to see my brother diving at the foot of a forsythia bush.

"Grub," I said, not shouting this time. He paid no attention. He dug at the ground under the bush from his knees, then stuffed something in his pocket.

What the hell . . . ?

I watched my brother dart across the yard to a flowerpot, which he threw to the ground. It shattered. He grabbed something from the spilled soil.

"Stop it, what are you doing?" I said, but he continued to ignore me, running to a short wall of landscaping stones. He flipped one over and grabbed something.

"Grub, stop!"

He didn't listen. I ran after him, wondering how I'd explain this to Dylan or his sister if they glanced out the window. Grub yanked a bird feeder from its hook, then tipped it upside down, spilling the seeds on the grass.

Now I was mad.

"Grub! Stop, dammit!" I spun him by his shoulder, and he let out a cry. I squeezed his wrist. "Give it to me."

I pried open his fingers. My breath caught in my throat.

In the palm of his hand lay a gold ring with tiny red jewels surrounded by the words *Class of '42.*

THIRTY-TWO

I EXAMINED THE RING WITH ONE HAND WHILE STILL HOLDING MY brother's wrist with the other. I felt confused. I felt angry. I also feared for my brother—how would I explain this to anyone?

"What are you doing with this?" I asked.

He hesitated. "It's one of the treasures."

I squeezed my eyes shut and shook my head. "*Treasures?* Grub, this is Letty's ring. Did you take it from her room?"

He looked down at the grass. "I was following Blackjack's orders."

"Blackjack's *orders?*" I clenched my jaw to keep my head from exploding. "Grub, you can't take people's things! This is real life!" It took all my willpower to keep from completely letting loose on him, but he looked scared enough as it was. "Why didn't you tell me?"

Grub sniffled. "It was supposed to be a top-secret mission. Blackjack told me about it that one day, when Rose was upset. You went to go see her and I stayed at Hilltop, remember? Blackjack told me not to tell anyone, that it was really important. But he's been sick ever since and I had to do it all by myself. Last night was the final mission."

My stomach sank to my ankles.

Mom was going to kill me. She told me I'd been self-involved this summer, and here was the proof. I should've been looking after my brother, but I'd been too distracted by my new girlfriend, my new band, my new *life*.

How long had Grub been stealing from residents? Three weeks? Longer? How many times had he talked about his "secret mission," or wandered Hilltop while I hung out in the common room?

I scanned Dylan's backyard—the bush, the flowerpot, the landscaping stones, the bird feeder—and suddenly remembered Grub's map with the circled Xs and Agatha standing guard.

Grub had been hiding stolen property in Dylan's backyard for weeks, right under my nose.

I stuffed Letty's ring in my pocket. "What else do you have? Give me all of it." Grub emptied his pockets, revealing earrings, necklaces, rare coins, and other assorted trinkets. I wanted to grab him and shake some sense into him, but I didn't. I shoved everything into my own pockets before anyone could see. I placed my hands on his shoulders and looked him in the eye.

I tried not to sound angry, even though I was. "What were you thinking?"

Grub's voice trembled. "I don't know why Blackjack got so mad. I took his medals last night, just like he told me. I had to hide them until I could bring them here."

Blackjack ordered Grub to take his medals, and doesn't remember doing it.

And then I found them in Mary's locker.

I felt like I'd just stuffed live grenades in my shorts. "Let's go. We're returning everything right *now.*"

"No!" Grub grabbed my shirt. "You have to give them to Rose."

I shut my eyes and squeezed the bridge of my nose, trying to make sense of what he'd said. "Grub, what are you talking about?"

"So she can pay for piano school." His chin trembled. "That's the top-secret mission."

My bones turned to jelly, and I collapsed to my knees in front of him. I looked into his brown eyes, glassy with tears. Grub had been trying to help Rose by *stealing* while I was supposed to be watching him.

And Blackjack . . .

His memory, his decline. He must not have known what he was saying.

How would I ever explain this to Mom?

Or Missy Stouffer.

Shit.

What was I going to do, march him back to Hilltop and turn him in? As if Missy Stouffer would say, "All right, that's settled, everyone have a great day!"

"Don't tell Blackjack I told you," begged Grub, his cheeks wet with tears. "I don't want him to get mad at me again. He said no one would get mad if we kept it a secret."

"No one's mad, Grub, but—"

Just then, Agatha bounded around the corner of the garage, followed by Dylan.

"What's up, dudes—whoa! What happened here?" Dylan said as he noticed the aftermath of Grub's backyard foraging.

"I'm sorry, man, I'll explain later," I said, though I wasn't sure how.

"Maggie's flowerpot! Oh man, she's gonna be *pissed*!"

Grub turned pale. He took three strained breaths, then curled over. He heaved, but nothing came out. His breaths became ragged, and he fell to the ground, shaking.

"Hey, whoa, it isn't *that* big a deal," said Dylan.

I knelt at Grub's side and put a hand on his shoulder. Agatha lay beside Grub and licked his face. "Hey, bud, we have to go take care of this, okay?" I said.

"I want to go home," he said between shallow breaths.

I sighed. "Okay, okay," I said. "I'll get you home."

And then I'll take care of this myself.

I turned to Dylan. "Any chance I can borrow your car?"

"Sure, man. Of course." He looked mildly alarmed.

"Thanks, I owe you one."

Grub lay silent in the back seat as I drove us across town. I'd figure things out once I got him home.

As soon as we walked in the door, Grub collapsed on our couch and curled into a tiny ball. I wrapped him in a blanket and sat beside him. His color had returned, though he was still visibly shaken. I decided I'd sit with him until Mom got back, then I'd return the stolen items. Problem solved.

Grub was almost asleep when his eyes flew open. "Don't tell Mom," he said, his voice panicky.

"Grub, we *have* to tell Mom. Don't worry, she won't be mad at you."

She'll be mad at me, I thought.

"But she'll be sad," Grub said. "Promise you won't tell her."

"Grub—" I began, then stopped and rubbed my eyes. He was right. Mom *would* be sad. Her business was failing, and now *both* her kids had screwed up big-time. Mom would be heartbroken. I didn't want to face that any more than Grub did.

"Promise me," Grub begged. "Don't tell *anyone*."

I tried to find part of him beneath the blanket to put my hand on, but he was so small. I found a foot. "Don't worry, I'll fix everything."

Grub soon fell asleep. I stared at the ceiling and considered the best way to return the stolen property. After an hour of deliberation, I felt like I had three options: (1) tell Missy Stouffer the truth and hope for the best; (2) sneak back to Hilltop in the middle of the night and leave everything in a box by the front door; or (3) have the stolen items shipped there anonymously, postmarked from Zanzibar.

Who was I kidding? The only real solution was to walk in there as soon as Mom got home and tell Missy the truth. She'd have to understand—Grub was only eight years old. If that meant both of us being banned from Hilltop, so be it.

It was the right thing to do.

I heard the locks turn, then Mom walked through the door. I put a finger to my lips and motioned to Grub, who slept soundly. Mom winked and headed for the kitchen. I'd tell her I needed to run somewhere quick and that I'd be right back.

Mom appeared a moment later holding my ringing phone. "It's Dylan," she said.

I took it and walked outside to the front steps for privacy. "Hello?"

"Hey, man, is everything all right? How's the little guy?"

"Better, thanks. Weird shit at the nursing home. Long story. Sorry about the flowerpot."

"Hey, don't worry about it. I told Maggie it was the squirrels. So what's going on at Hilltop? Cops were there a little while ago."

I yanked the phone away from my ear and stared at it. I

could hear Dylan's distant voice saying, "You there? Hello?" I felt my vision blacking out from the sides and had to sit down.

Missy already called the police.

"I'll call you back," I said, then hung up.

I sat there debating what to do next. Why didn't I return everything when I had the chance? Now the police were involved. I looked at my bulging pockets and suddenly felt like a criminal. I scanned left and right down our street, paranoid, fully expecting to see blue-and-red flashing lights heading straight for me. I took a few deep breaths to slow my heart rate.

Rose.

I called her number. She answered on the first ring. "Zeus?"

"Rose. Are you okay?"

Silence. Then a sound. Crying. "What the hell is going on, Zeus?"

"What do you mean?" Silence. Rose sniffed. "What is it?" I asked.

"Where did you go? I had to talk to a detective earlier."

I felt like I was losing my mind. "What?"

"My mom did too."

"Why'd Missy call the cops?"

"I don't know. It doesn't matter. It's too late now. A criminal record will look great on my college applications."

"Wait, what? What happened? They arrested you?" I supported my forehead with my free hand.

"No." She took a deep, shaky breath. "But they interviewed everyone. And Blackjack told the detective my mom and I stole everything."

"What!? The detective didn't believe him, did he? Rose, he has *Alzheimer's*!"

"I know that! But none of the other missing property has been found yet. And you found his medals in my mom's locker! How were we supposed to explain that?"

I felt the items digging into my legs as I spoke. I squeezed my eyes shut at the lie. Then I almost puked at the truth.

"Rose, don't worry. I'll take care of it."

"You'll take care of it?"

"I will."

Rose paused. "How? Missy suspended me and my mom without pay until this gets cleared up. My mom is a wreck. Not only about her job, but about Blackjack, too. He's really sick. I don't know what we're going to do."

"Oh God, Rose," I said, standing up again abruptly. "I'm so sorry."

"The detective said he wants to talk to you. Grub, too. When he asked where you were, someone told him they saw you two run out the front door."

My hands and feet went cold, despite it being a hot August night. I wiped the sweat from my forehead, then grabbed my hair in a fist. Ripping it all out would have felt better than the guilt coursing through me.

There was only one thing to do.

"I'll take care of everything, I promise," I said.

I hung up and started walking.

I walked and I walked, rehearsing what I'd say.

I entered the police station and asked to speak with an officer.

THIRTY-THREE

THE CAMERA IN THE CEILING CORNER STARED AT ME, ITS RED EYE unblinking. I wondered if I was being recorded. Probably. I tried to control my breathing. I'd never been in any *real* trouble in my life. But things hadn't gone as planned.

My *plan* had been to hand over the missing property, explain how I'd found it on the street, then walk out of there. Simple as that.

Or so I'd thought.

Fifteen minutes later I sat in an interrogation room awaiting a detective.

"He just wants to ask you a few questions," the first officer had said after he'd taken my statement. "Wanna call your parents, have them meet you down here while you're waiting?"

"No, thanks," I replied, trying to look more confident than I felt.

"You sure?"

"Yes, sir. My mom's at home with my little brother. I'll fill her in when I get back."

"If you insist."

Nearly an hour passed.

What was taking so long? I rubbed my hands together to keep them warm in the overly air-conditioned room. I bounced my knees up and down. Rose called. Twice. Three times. Mom called a few times too. Dylan texted. I didn't answer any of them. I'd explain later.

Finally, the door opened, making me jump.

A man wearing jeans and a black polo shirt walked in, a Styrofoam cup of coffee in one hand, a manila folder in the other. A lanyard and badge hung from his neck. On his hip, a gun. He appeared to be in his forties, with short salt-and-pepper hair and gray stubble on a chiseled jawline. I'd seen him before. It was the cop from the Open Mic.

He dropped the folder on the table between us.

"Mr. Gunderson," he said without looking at me. He sat across the table and opened the folder. I couldn't believe this was the same guy who'd sung "American Girl" at the Beauty Saloon.

"Hi." My voice sounded like someone else's. Higher, weaker.

The detective flipped through the folder for a moment

before speaking. "I'm Detective Van Reusch." Another long pause as he scanned a piece of paper from top to bottom. "No parent here with you? Lawyer?"

"No, sir. I'm not in trouble, am I?"

The detective looked up at me, but didn't reply. The silence was deafening.

"I thought—" My words caught in my throat. I began to wonder if I'd made a huge mistake. "I just wanted to turn in the stuff I found. Do I need to have a lawyer or parent here?"

Detective Van Reusch sat back and folded his hands. "No, although you do have that right. I was told you walked in here of your own accord. Is that correct?"

"Yes, sir."

"Well then, you're free to leave anytime," he said, motioning toward the door. "I just have a few questions."

"Okay."

He held up the paper he was looking at and showed it to me. "Officer Higgerson informed me you found these items. Is that correct?"

"Yes."

Detective Van Reusch nodded. "On the sidewalk?"

"Yes."

"Just stumbled upon them?"

"Yes, sir."

He nodded again. "And are you aware these items were

reported stolen from Hilltop Nursing Home earlier this evening?"

I blinked. "I just found everything in the box and turned it in right away."

Detective Van Reusch rubbed his chin and scanned the report. "So let me get this timeline straight. Property gets stolen from the residents of Hilltop Nursing Home, everything gets placed in a box, and then you find it on the sidewalk a couple hours later and turn it in." He shot his eyes up at me. "That correct?"

"Correct."

"Uh-huh." Another long pause. "Tell me, Mr. Gunderson, were you at Hilltop Nursing Home earlier today?"

My stomach dropped. I remembered what Rose had said on the phone. *"The detective said he wants to talk to you . . . someone told him they saw you two run out the front door."*

I hadn't figured out an explanation for that part of the story yet. My mind raced, trying to come up with some plausible reason for running out of Hilltop.

"It's a simple question. Were you at Hilltop Nursing Home earlier today?"

"Uh, yes."

Detective Van Reusch took a deep breath and leaned forward on his elbows. "So was I. In fact, I took this report," he said, wagging the folder at me.

I swallowed. My tongue felt dry and swollen.

"Look, multiple witnesses saw you and your brother running away shortly before I arrived. And that lovely director, Ms. Stouffer, said it was *you* who found Mr. Porter's medals. Now, I'm not saying you stole the property." He paused to take a sip of his coffee. "But innocent people don't run." He let that sink in a while before continuing. "Are you sticking with your story?"

This isn't going well. Why hadn't I told Mom the truth, or just returned everything right away? I knew I was standing on thin ice. But I couldn't change my story now. That'd look even worse.

"Yes, sir. That's how it happened. I found the box on the sidewalk," I replied.

"Mm-hmm." The detective took another sip of coffee and grimaced as he swallowed it. "Mr. Gunderson, I've been doing this a long time. In my line of work, we call your story *suspicious.* Some might even say you're interfering with an official police investigation by giving false information. Are you telling me the truth, Mr. Gunderson?"

By now, I felt certain the detective could see my heart thudding beneath my T-shirt. I began to speak, but nothing came out.

Detective Van Reusch continued. "That's what I thought. Personally, I don't think you stole the property yourself. But I think you know who did. Who are you covering for?"

I closed my eyes and took a deep breath.

I heard Grub crying earlier. *Don't tell Mom . . . promise me. Don't tell* anyone.

I heard Mom. *There's nothing wrong with that boy, do you hear me?*

Rose. *I don't know what we're going to do.*

Me. *I'll take care of everything, I promise.*

I couldn't back down now.

I opened my eyes and cleared my throat. "I didn't just find those things on the sidewalk, I took them myself," I said. "No one else had anything to do with it."

Detective Van Reusch tilted his head and studied me for several seconds. "Now you're saying *you* took everything?"

I nodded.

"You, a kid with no criminal record—no motive at all, in fact—stole jewelry from nursing home residents?"

My new story didn't sound very convincing to me either. But I was sixteen, a minor. How bad could the punishment be? I found a spot on the table to stare at.

"Mr. Gunderson, depending on the value of these items, this could be a class two felony. Grand larceny. And if you're covering for someone else, that won't go well for you either."

Felony.

Larceny.

Jail.

"You want to tell me what really happened, son?"

Suddenly, I *did* want to tell him, but I could hardly piece it all together. The truth had been twisted and turned and stretched into something unrecognizable . . .

An old man's shattered memory.

A young boy's misguided game.

An older brother's neglect.

I shut my eyes and tried to concentrate. After a minute, I took a deep breath and spoke.

"I need to start at the beginning."

Detective Van Reusch leaned in. "Please."

Early the next morning, I drove Dylan's car across the bridge to return it, my bike sticking out of the trunk. I'd only slept a few hours. Grub stayed home with Mom, who'd closed the café for the day. From Dylan's house, I'd ride to Hilltop and explain everything to Missy, then from there, to Rose's.

This time, I'd tell everyone the truth.

The truth I'd told Detective Van Reusch the night before.

The truth I'd told Mom when I got home.

She'd taken it well—as well as could be expected, anyway. We'd sat on the front steps and talked into the wee hours of the morning. The birds were chirping by the time we went inside. Apologies were featured heavily throughout the night, not only from me, but from Mom, too. After giving me a full dressing down for going to the police station on my own, she cried, and then her accusations turned inward, blaming herself for everything that had happened.

I insisted it was my fault, that I should have paid more attention, but she insisted it was her fault, that she'd been too distracted by the café to be a proper mother to her sons. After a bit of back and forth, we finally decided that no matter who was to blame, we all needed to spend more quality time with one another, especially with Grub.

We were a family. A small one, perhaps, but that was even more of a reason to stick together, whatever happened next.

And that was still a toss-up.

The night before, Detective Van Reusch had told me he'd be returning the stolen property to Hilltop the next day. "I need to confer with Ms. Stouffer before we determine the next course of action. It's her facility, and her right to press criminal charges. But given the circumstances, I myself am inclined to call it a misunderstanding."

"Thank you, Detective," I'd said, shaking his hand. He'd been more than fair with me, and I was grateful.

Mom and I both agreed I should talk to Ms. Stouffer first thing, to apologize. If she agreed not to press charges, the whole thing could be dropped. Grub and I would probably never be allowed in Hilltop again, but hopefully everyone else would be cleared, and Mary and Rose could return to their jobs. I'd miss all the staff and residents, of course, more than I wanted to admit. Letty especially.

At least she'd get her husband's class ring back.

I was hoping Ms. Stouffer—if she wasn't too mad after I told her the truth—would let me see Letty real quick, to explain.

But first, I had to drop off Dylan's car. I owed him an explanation as well.

As I approached Dylan's house, flashing lights to the north caught my eye. The parking lot at Hilltop.

Police again?

I slowed down.

Ambulance.

I flew past Dylan's house and headed for Hilltop, remembering Rose's words the day before. *My mom is a wreck. Not only about her job, but about Blackjack, too. He's really sick.*

I parked the car and ran toward the emergency vehicle, its lights still flashing. Just then, Hilltop's glass doors slid open and paramedics rolled out a body on a stretcher.

The face was covered.

Oh God. Please don't be Blackjack, I prayed. *Not after all this.*

Missy Stouffer walked behind the stretcher. She looked surprised to see me. Then her expression turned to one I'd never seen before: pity.

"I'm so sorry, Zeus."

I hung my head. "I'll let my brother know. He really loved Mr. Porter." I turned to leave.

"Zeus . . ."

I looked back. "Yeah?"

"It's Letty Kowalczyk. She died in her sleep."

THIRTY-FOUR

THEY'RE IN A BETTER PLACE NOW. SHE'S NOT IN PAIN ANYMORE. HE LIVED a good, long life.

The useless euphemisms and pleasantries we tell ourselves when someone dies, to make sense of it.

Passed on. Crossed over. Entered the Sweet Hereafter.

Dead. Forever. Gone.

Letty was gone, two days past ninety.

After sitting in Dylan's car for thirty minutes, I drove to Rose's. I was still stunned, and so were Rose and Mary when I told them the news. How could a person be so *alive* one day, then gone the next? I guess it should've made me feel better knowing that Letty had lived a long, happy life, and that she'd now "crossed over" to some grand party in the sky. But instead I felt hollow and broken. And incredibly sad.

Once we'd recovered from the initial shock, Mary made us tea. Then I swallowed my grief and told them about everything else—Grub, Blackjack, the top-secret mission, the police station—all of it.

"So that's why you didn't answer your phone last night," Rose murmured, placing her hand over mine. "We were worried about you."

"I'm sorry, Rose. And you too, Mary. I should've been watching Grub more carefully. And now your jobs are at stake. I'm so sorry," I repeated.

"You can't blame yourself, Zeus," Mary said. "I missed the signs, too. Grub made Blackjack so happy this summer, happier than he's been in years. I allowed them both more freedom than I should have. We all did."

"But Ms. Stouffer has to understand that, doesn't she?" Rose asked. "Nobody did anything wrong on purpose."

"No," Mary agreed. "And certainly not Grub. How's he doing, Zeus? This all must have been so frightening for him."

"He's a little shaken up. Mom and I are going to talk to him today about what happened. Speaking of that, I should get going. Thanks for the tea."

"Talk soon?" Rose asked.

I smiled at her. "Talk soon."

I hugged Rose and Mary good-bye, dropped the car off at

Dylan's with a quick promise to explain things later, then pedaled home.

I filled Mom in privately on the events of the morning. She knew how close I'd grown to Letty, and offered her best consolation. Later, we took Grub out for ice cream. We both reassured him that nobody was mad at him, but we also talked about Blackjack's illness and how sometimes it made his brain play tricks on him.

Grub blinked back tears. "Does that mean I can't play army with him anymore? I thought we were just pretending."

"You can still play army and pretend, Manny. But your brother and I need you here in the real world, too," said Mom, running a finger down his cheek. The cell phone buzzed in her purse. She took it out and frowned. "I'll be right back."

Grub glanced at me as she walked away, his face creased with worry.

"Mom's not mad or sad, Grub, she's just concerned," I explained, remembering a certain conversation earlier that summer. "It's what moms do. It's her job to worry about us. I promise."

Grub picked the blue, red, and green gummy bears out of his vanilla ice cream, leaving only the yellow ones. "You promised me before. You promised you wouldn't tell anyone."

"I know I did. Listen, about that . . ."

He looked up at me then, his brown eyes solemn.

"Sometimes keeping secrets is a bad thing," I continued.

"What do you mean?"

I searched for an example he'd understand. "Like with Blackjack. He made you promise not to tell anyone about the secret mission, but eventually you told me. And it was the right thing to do."

Grub thought for a moment. "How do you know when something's the right thing to do?"

I gave him a soft pat on the shoulder, then rubbed the back of his neck. "It's not always easy. Sometimes you'll do the wrong thing, and people will be mad at you. Other times you'll say the wrong thing and make someone sad. And then sometimes nothing will make any sense at all and it will seem like, no matter what you do, you're making the wrong choice."

Grub played with his ice cream for a minute, thinking. "That sounds complicated."

"It is. But the important thing is, you can always trust *me*, Grub. And I'll always trust you. We're brothers, right?"

He turned and smiled at me. Melted ice cream ringed his mouth. "Right."

"Good news," Mom said, bustling back over. "That was Detective Van Reusch. All the property has been returned to the owners, and Ms. Stouffer isn't pressing charges. The whole case is being dropped! Apparently neither she nor the police want rumors floating around that Hilltop Nursing Home isn't a safe, secure facility for its residents."

"Thank God," I said, blowing air out of my cheeks. "What about Mary and Rose?"

"No longer suspended."

I felt a twenty-pound weight lift from my chest.

For the next four days, I didn't leave the house or see anyone besides Mom and Grub. Mom decided to close the café until after Letty's memorial service, which was set for Saturday. I exchanged a few texts with Dylan and let Axl and Novie know how sorry I was for the loss of their great-grandmother. Rose and I talked on the phone before bed every night, but we didn't see each other. I'd see everyone soon enough.

Meanwhile, I needed time with my family.

Time with Grub.

Time to myself, to grieve for Letty.

Mom, Grub, and I spent a lot of time looking through old pictures, reminiscing, and simply enjoying one another's company. It felt like old times. We talked about growing up and growing old and everything that happens in between. We also played about two dozen games of Battleship. Grub won every time.

By the time Saturday arrived, it felt good to get out of our apartment and breathe fresh air. Letty's memorial service was held at one of the old churches in downtown Buffalo Falls. As we walked in, I squinted at the peak of the tallest steeple, which looked as if it were trying to pierce the clouds.

Inside the church, the air buzzed with conversation. Dylan played instrumental acoustic guitar in the corner. The pews had already filled, so we found open space to stand in the back along with dozens of others. I recognized several familiar faces: the Larsens, Candy, Vera, the Bettys. I spotted Axl and Novie's white-blond hair near the front with the rest of their family. I looked for Rose in the sea of people but couldn't find her.

While we waited for the service to begin, I wandered over to a display of photographs. I looked at black-and-white glamour shots of Letty as a young woman, a wedding photo of her and Dickey, and numerous others of her surrounded by her enormous family.

The most recent picture was from her ninetieth birthday party. I picked it up for a closer look. Someone must have stood on a table at Hilltop to get an overhead angle. It was a shot of the entire dance floor. I could make out the band off to the side looking, well, like a *real* band.

In the center, a flash of gold, a cone-shaped party hat, and pure joy.

I heard Letty's voice in my head, her cackling laugh. *Enjoy today, kid, you might be dead tomorrow!*

It brought a smile to my face.

The service began with a minister reading passages from the Bible, then addressing the congregation and making vague statements about Letty's life—all the things one might expect at a memorial service. Honestly, it didn't feel Letty-like at all.

But after that, a cordless microphone was passed around, and one by one people began to share their memories of Letty. While there were plenty of funny stories about Letty's escapades—her love of dancing, her sense of humor, her infectious laugh—just as many were told of her kindness. The way she'd feed any kid in the neighborhood who needed a meal, even with five kids of her own. The way she volunteered at the community soup kitchen for years and turned every meal into a party. The way she always seemed to know when someone needed a friend.

Vera spoke, telling the story of her first day at Hilltop and how scared and lonely she'd felt. She'd sat in her room and cried that night, until Letty sprang in with a grin and a checkerboard to cheer her up.

"Letty found a reason to be happy every day of her life until the very end," Vera concluded. "We should all live so well."

Letty's granddaughter, Crash, took the microphone then. After sharing a few stories of her own, she thanked everyone for coming and ended by directly addressing Letty's casket, which had been covered in wildflowers.

"One last thing, Grandma." Crash pulled a small flask from her pocket and held it in the air. The crowd murmured and laughed. "Here's to you. Here's to living life *your* way. You knew how to have a good time like nobody else. I'd pour one out for you, Grandma, but I know what you'd say—'That's a waste of a good drink!'" Everyone laughed, a few people clapped, and a couple even hooted. "So I'll drink yours for you. We're all going to miss you, Letty Kowalczyk. Cheers!"

I laughed and clapped along with the rest of the room. As the noise subsided, Dylan resumed playing guitar and people began to disperse. I scanned the crowd but still couldn't see Rose.

I felt a hand on my shoulder and turned.

"Hello, Zeus."

"Hello, Ms. Stouffer."

We stood looking at each other in awkward silence. I realized two things about Hilltop's director in that moment: (1) death was an unfortunate but common job-related hazard for her; and (2) she didn't enjoy it any more than the rest of us.

"Thank you," she finally said, "for returning everything. Detective Van Reusch let me read the police report. I found it very enlightening."

"You did?"

Missy paused a moment, as if she struggled to say the next words. "Mr. Porter—Blackjack—may never know what you did to protect his dignity, but I will. The whole situation was very unfortunate. As a result, the staff and I have established a few new rules to protect everyone's well-being, volunteers included."

My eyes shot to the ground. *Here comes the lifetime ban from Hilltop.*

"That said, we'd love to have you back at Hilltop, Zeus. Your brother, too."

I glanced back up and tried to find words to thank her, but I was too shocked to produce any.

"One more thing," Missy added. "Letty's wearing her husband's class ring. Family decision. I thought you'd like to know she got it back." Then she smiled. I almost told her she should try it more often. I almost shook her hand. Hell, I almost hugged her, but she turned to leave, and I just stood there grinning.

Suddenly, Dylan played the opening flurry of notes to "She's a Lady" and began to sing. The Bettys, the Larsens, Vera, and several other Hilltoppers stopped in their tracks upon hearing Letty's favorite Tom Jones song and began dancing with one another at the back of the church. Letty's family joined in, and soon what seemed like the entire population of Buffalo Falls belted out the chorus. *"She's a lady! Whoa, whoa, whoa, she's a lady!"*

Letty would have loved it. Maybe, in fact, she was clapping along that very moment from her dance party in the sky.

After the song wound down, Crash approached Mom. "Coriander, I can't stop thinking about those brownies of yours. Oh. My. God. Listen, I have a Christmas party every year at the Beauty Saloon. There's usually a hundred people there, and a lot of them are local business owners. I'm thinking: you, me, a bottle of wine, and some tacos. Then we brainstorm and come up with a menu. What do you say?"

Mom glanced at me with an expression I understood—things were looking up. "I think that sounds wonderful!" she said, squeezing Grub, who stood in front of her. He and I winked at each other.

Just then I spotted Rose, who waved and nodded toward the exit.

"Be right back," I said.

Mom smiled, ruffled my hair, then returned to her conversation with Crash.

Around the side of the church lay a sprawling green lawn, recently mown. An arched trellis consumed by morning glories led to a cobblestoned clearing where Rose sat upon a stone bench. "Hey stranger," she said.

"Hey," I said softly, sitting beside her. I took her hand and pulled her into me. She leaned her head on my shoulder. That familiar feeling I'd been missing returned. I rubbed the back of her hand with my thumb while we sat in comfortable silence.

"How's Grub doing?" she finally asked.

"He's okay, but sad, too. He misses Blackjack and Hilltop, although Missy Stouffer just informed me she'd love to have us back, if you can believe it."

Rose lifted her head from my chest. "That's great, Zeus!"

"I know. It'll be different without Letty there, but we'll still have fun." I squeezed her hand. "Maybe we can learn a new song for the Christmas party."

She hesitated, then sat up straight to look at me. Something flickered in her eyes. Apprehension, maybe. "Zeus, I need to tell you something."

My stomach clenched, though I tried to keep my expression open, inviting her next words. "What is it?"

Rose bit her lip. "My dad's coming through with the money for school. I can go now. To New York."

I stared back at her as a million thoughts raced through my mind.

"I haven't said yes yet," Rose said, her voice catching.

The whole summer flashed before my eyes—the Sunday surprises, Hilltop, Old Dump Road. Every conversation, every glance, every touch. All the time I'd spent thinking, wondering, daydreaming about Rose. My family. White light. All that I'd done—right, wrong, and everything in between.

And then I remembered the last thing Letty had told me: *Remember the good stuff, kiddo. Nothing else matters.*

I threw my arms around Rose. "You have to say yes!" I released her and held her by the shoulders. "This is your dream, this is what you've been waiting for!"

"I know it is," Rose said, her eyes shiny with tears. "But what about you?"

"Me? I'll roll up in the fetal position for a while until I find the will to live. It shouldn't take long, maybe a few months." I smiled. "I'll be fine. You'll be fine. You'll be *amazing*. You have to go, Rose, you know you do. Seriously."

She smiled big, bringing out the dimple below her lip. "You're the best, Zeus. *Seriously.*"

In all honesty, I don't remember what I said next. I don't need to though. As far as memories go, it's one of the good ones, and nothing else matters.

For the next two weeks, Rose and I spent every possible moment together. I helped her pack, and we read through all her books on New York City. Grub and I continued our volunteer visits to Hilltop. Blackjack slept a lot, but he still seemed to enjoy his comrade's company at his bedside.

The night before Rose left for New York, we lay on a blanket at Old Dump Road holding hands and watching the stars.

"This was the best summer of my life," Rose said.

"Mine, too. Sorry I screwed it up there at the end."

"Oh, stop. What you did was very brave." Rose kissed me. "*You're* very brave."

I squeezed her hand. "No, I'm not. There's one thing I haven't told you yet."

Rose turned toward me. "So tell me."

"Not now. But someday, Rose. I promise."

Someday I'd tell her.

Someday I'd have the words.

THIRTY-FIVE

December 23

Dear Rose,

How's the weather in the Big Apple? (And why do people call it that, anyway?) I bet your dad and family are glad to have you show them around the city for the holidays. You must be an expert tour guide by now.

As for Buffalo Falls, we got slammed with six inches of snow yesterday. I took Grub and his new friend, Foster, sledding down the big hill at the park. They rode bazooka, Nerf guns and all. Remember our afternoons there by the river?

I just got back from the Beauty Saloon, where World

Peas Café catered a party. It's funny how even though I was surrounded by people, I couldn't stop thinking about you. Mom got to debut her newest creation, *All I Want for Christmas Is Tiramisu*, and the band played Christmas songs. Crash gave us a whopping fifty dollars to play—our first paid gig! We're actually getting pretty decent.

I think Crash has single-handedly saved Mom's business with these catering jobs. I swear, that woman knows everyone in this town. Missy Stouffer even showed up to the party with her new boyfriend, Detective Van Reusch. They call me their criminal cupid, ha. In other small-town-romance news, Dylan's new girlfriend, Kaylee, was there, and I invited your friend Tracie, whom Novie was crushing on all night, so Buffalo Falls may have another "cutest couple" soon. And Axl just upgraded to a brand-new five-string bass, which I'm pretty sure is a love affair all its own.

I still see your mom every weekday at Hilltop. I'm sure she told you that Blackjack was moved into hospice care last week. Grub stops in often and draws maps at his bedside, but Blackjack is rarely lucid anymore. He does seem comforted by Grub's visits though. Grub's made friends and is doing well, but he meets regularly with the school psychologist to help him process what happened last summer and understand Blackjack's illness.

I spend my time at Hilltop with my new pal, Vera,

playing Scrabble and checkers. Everyone misses your piano playing there, me most of all. Dylan and I bring our guitars sometimes, but we have big shoes to fill.

Anyway, I know I'm a little late, but I haven't forgotten about my promise, the one thing I never told you:

You were the first girl I ever loved, Rose, the girl who taught me to enjoy today, even if it meant tomorrow might hurt. I wouldn't exchange a single day.

No matter where you are—here, there, everywhere—you'll always be the first, Rose.

The first everything.

Merry Christmas, Miss Santos.

Love, Zeus

ACKNOWLEDGMENTS

Our deepest appreciation to Catherine Wallace, for pushing us to find the heart of this story, and her patience while we did so.

We're also indebted to Kristen Pettit and the talented HarperTeen gang for all their behind-the-scenes magic to turn our words into a real live book.

Heartfelt thanks as well to the home team:

To our agents, Tracey and Josh Adams—for being the best at what you do!

To our early readers—Joe and Bonnie Terrones, Kyle Durango, Peter Kousathanas, Sherry Stanford, and Diane Stevenson—for cheering us on and laughing in all the right places.

To Ryan Durango, map-maker extraordinaire, World War II buff, and our inspiration for young Grub. *Pew-pew!*

To Cheryl Pollard, for generously sharing her beautiful cottage on Geneva Lake. We can't imagine a better writing, research, and relaxation retreat. (Or hostess!)

To Santiago Durango, for advising us on the criminal justice system (all literary crimes are our own) and his punk-rock badassery in general.

To Hillary Stanford, for Chopin's *Raindrop Prelude* and her incredible piano talent.

To Annabel Tomás, RN, and her father, Arturo Tomás, MD, for their dedicated work in the medical field and for double-checking our Tagalog. *Salamat!*

To Larry and Susan Greider, Angie and Mike Stevenson, Jenny Cottingham, Tracie Vaughn Kleman, Pat Sauber, Paul Higgerson, Katie Belle and the Belle Rangers, and our extended family and friends, for your ongoing enthusiasm and support throughout the process. Your love and friendship mean the world to us.